POPPY

POPPY

A Modern-Day Courtesan

David J. Nowel

THE REGENCY
PUBLISHERS

ISBN: 978-1-957724-38-6 (Paperback Edition)
ISBN: 978-1-957724-37-9 (Hardcover Edition)
ISBN: 978-1-957724-39-3 (E-book Edition)

Book Ordering Information

Phone Number: 315-537-3088
Email: info@theregencypublishers.com
The Regency Publishers, US
www.theregencypublishers.us

Printed in the United States of America

Book One
The Hang Out Girl

Book Two
Poppy's Sexuality

The End

In memory of

Lynn Nowel Bradshaw Daughter self-inflicted asphyxiation age 43

Neil Ginnetti Childhood and longtime friend died of a massive heart attack, one year after retirement Age 62

Philip Flegel Lifetime friend died of spleen cancer age53

Nancy Sparks Lifetime friend died of leukemia age 51

Sophie Boswell (BUNTY) Artistic friend died of leukemia age 71

Helene Becker College Girl Friend and lifetime friend died autoimmune complications Age 82

Marilyn Hickman High School Sweetheart died from leukemia Age 19

Dedication

Solana Nowel, My Youngest Granddaughter

Dean Del Giudice

Gay Matheson

Miles Nowel (My Youngest Grandson)

Chloe (Agent)

The questions I was asking while writing this story. What is love? How much of our love is based on possessiveness? Would the world be a better place if we were less possessive?

Somehow, I do believe that in the future, as we live longer; we humans will develop a better balance between our love and possessiveness.

Preface

I really believe that our childhood experiences will determine what will become the backbone for our adult development. I even believe that as a fetus; we receive certain impressions of the world outside of our mother's comforting environment. Those impressions will affect us in our later life. We know that a child can recognize whether he is a male or female. That condition occurs within the first six months after we are born. All children, within those six months, they determine whether they are male or female.

So, I wrote three complete chapters on the relationship that Poppy had with her father, but after considering the sensitivity of our society to this topic; it might be interpreted as inappropriate.

Since this is a novel and not a case history, I understand the delicacy of that kind of discussion; therefore, I have decided not to include those three chapters in this novel.

Needlessly, something happened. We know it wasn't incestual. Maybe more of mentoring relationship. We do know that she admired him.

We also know that Poppy decided to leave home at a ripe young age of fourteen and move to Las Vegas. With help from friends, she began her successful career as a professional____ A High-Priced Escort. It is much later that she becomes Poppy, who I am writing about: A Modern-Day Courtesan. There is no question that she had an infinity for older men who reminded her of her father.

Book One

The Hang Out Girl

Chapter 1

The First Meeting

The restaurant emptied out fast. It was getting close to starting time. Everybody was leaving and running across the street to the Angel's Stadium. He and the fellow next to him had the whole bar to themselves. It was sort of an oval bar and it wrapped itself all the way around and you could see the faces of other people on the other side of the bar. Lots and lots of faces ____and that was only minutes ago. But now, there was just open space.

He started a conversation with the guy next to him.

"Boy that was pretty quick. The place was wall to wall people and now it's just you and me."

While drinking his beer, the stranger said. "Oh, I'm just waiting for my date. She knows the starting time. I hope she gets here soon. Well at least, we won't have to fight the crowd trying to get into Angel's Stadium."

Michael continued, "I did this newspaper dating thing and I am waiting for her. I don't know what she looks like, and she doesn't know what I look like, but she shouldn't have any trouble finding me. Now it's just you and me."

"How's that dating thing work? I wanted to try and do it, but I met this lady and things are working out."

Somewhat under his breath. "Except, I wish she was more punctual. She always seems to be running late. I don't want to miss too much of this game."

Michael trying to explain. "It's a Newspaper Dating Game_______ The whole thing is just another way to meet someone. I met someone that I liked a while back, doing something like this. But at that time, it was a magazine. This is a newspaper thing and something new for me; I liked the magazine better. Unfortunately, they went out of business. I think, this type of dating is a little better than doing the bar scene. I don't know about this newspaper thing because there aren't any pictures. With the magazine, the gals sent you lots of pictures to your post office box. I did talk to her on the phone, and she sounded sultry and sexy. I have learned to have the first date by usually offering to have a drink. In that way, you could have a conversation and see if it kicks off. If it works, you can go further. I did a supper thing at one time. It was total fiasco. Right in the beginning of the supper, we both hated each other and yet we had to stomach each other for another 45 minutes while we ate our food. We both couldn't wait to get the hell out of there. I made a mistake. I guess I didn't learn. I did it one more time.

This time she insisted we move because she was cold being at the bar. In the middle of the whole thing, she told me she still had a boyfriend, and she was trying to find out what was out there. You know, just in case, they broke up. She sucked me in, and she chose the most expensive thing on the menu. On top of that, she wasn't that great looking. You get a lot of that; some people are just putting out feelers at the guy's expense. Never will I do the supper think again."

At that moment, he saw a woman walking on the other side of the bar, nonchalantly, trying not to be noticed. She was checking them out. From what he could see, in just a flash of a second, he wasn't impressed.

He whispered to the guy. "I think this is going to turn out to be shortest date in my life."

Thinking to himself, he was starting to be ashamed to be seen with such a homely woman.

He could see that she was confused. He didn't want any more embarrassments. To make it clear that he was her date and not the guy sitting next to him. He turned around to greet her, now facing her.

"You must be Poppy. I saw you coming from around the other end of the bar."

"I wasn't quite sure that it was you. Neither one of you fit the description in the newspaper."

She pulled out the clipping.

"It says here that you're 6' 4" tall and 51 years old"

He looked at the Ad and she was correct.

He missed the typo since he really didn't bother to check that field because he had concentrated on the main body of his Ad.

"It was supposed to read that I was 64 and 5" 11. I am sorry. I do lie about my age from time to time but not my height."

"I am just teasing you. I like older men and you are tall enough. But that's why I kept checking you out."

She had horrible skin. It looked like her whole face was on fire with acne or disfiguration from Smallpox. He came from a family of women who always admired how wonderful their skin looked. He was sure that this was going to be a very short date. He was so turned off and of course she felt it.

He didn't want to be mean. He was a salesman and always could put on a good mask and make people feel comfortable. She did look and act young. He guessed she was in her middle thirties although he knew from her stats that she was in her forties. He knew from their conversation on the phone, she was proud of the fact that she was thin, and that was no small accomplishment. So many people his age were overweight and that included himself.

He ordered her drink and they tried to talk about nothing. And as they were talking a new group of people started to appear. The restaurant was filling up rapidly.

He heard an announcement on the restaurant's P.A. System. "There are cars parked blocking the shipping docks. They are getting a late shipment and asking the owners of cars parked blocking the shipping areas to immediately move. Your cars will be towed, at the owner's expense."

He didn't know where the mix up occurred. He did go up to the hostess and start asking her questions about the parking situation. He asked her what area he should be worried about.

The hostess reassured him. "As long as your car is not in front of a loading dock. The loading docks are on the backside of the building and if you are parked in the front you don't have to worry, your car will be fine." The hostess insisted that he need not worry, and that announcement didn't affect anyone who was in the restaurants parking area.

He knew he didn't have to worry. When he got there, He was lucky. In front of him, someone was pulling out of a choice spot only feet from the front door. Yah, so he was parked up front.

He passed that information onto Poppy. He tried to explain all of that to her.

"Well, everything's cool as long as we're parked where we need to be and not parked in front of a loading dock. We don't have to worry about anything."

Chapter 2

Dancing

After their drinks, he was ready to call it a night.

They were walking out together. He wanted to at least pretend to be a gentleman and walk her to her car. He would say goodbye to her and that would be it.

"So, you're a nurse?

"Yes, I do intensive care. I like it because it is busy, and time goes by fast. My head nurse likes me and gives me good hours. I work twelve hours shifts, three days on and four days off. She sometimes gives me almost a whole week off. Sort of a mini vacation."

They had only walked a few feet when he heard the blaring of music. The place next door had dancing.

He decided why not?

"Hey, you want to try it out?"

He looked at her.

"You want to go in?"

She smiled and nodded her head. "Let's do it."

They both jumped into the place and into the sound of the blaring music.

Michael always liked dancing. From an early age, it was part of his background. His hometown was made up of mostly Polish factory laborers, who all seemed to work at Stanley Works. He didn't know whether he was from a town that was predominately made up of low middle class or low-class people. If he used the standard from his college experience, it was a mixture of low-class people with a touch of low middle. However, if he used the New Britain's Standards, he would have to say it was low middle. He might be able to meet those of the upper class and upper middle when he was a caddy at Shadow Meadow Country Club, but that was it. Of course, no Jews were allowed at that country club. He did meet some middle-class people in high school. At that time, there were no Blacks or Asians living in that town.

Even the religious mix of that town was confusing, there was the old Polish Catholic Church and there was the New Polish Catholic Church. There was the Old Italian Catholic Church and the new one. Catholics made up ninety percent of the population and socializing with Protestant or Jewish people were very limiting. As a Catholic, it was forbidden and a mortal sin to participate in either of their services.

There also were the Irish and they had an early advantage in being the first large wave of immigrants in New Britain. Most of the politicians, teachers, policemen, and firemen were Irish.

There was section next to the Italian ghetto that were made up of many small Jewish retail stores that were important to the residence. Sunday was a Holy Day reserved for praying and all catholic stores were closed but not those Jewish's stores. It was the only place to shop, and it was fun.

The Old Polish Church catered to those Poles that still felt some allegiance to their mother country, Poland. In their schools, the church taught the Polish language as well as their history and they encouraged their older traditions. Being the older or original church in that town, the monsignor accumulated a great deal of wealth for his congregation by buying property. The monsignor was a smart old man. Eventually, that church own a third of the land in New Britain. The land he bought was cheap. It bordered on the then wilderness part of the city and that resembled the topography of San Francisco's rolling hills. It was very inexpensive when it was purchased. It was in the northwest part of the city.

He did make good use of that land. He developed part of it into a large cemetery and that's one thing every city needed was a cemetery. After all, cemeteries were very profitable business. Everyone must be buried sooner or later. And he charged premium dollar for each burial site. Not to mention the profits from the stone monuments. While the rest of the land was eventually sold as subdivisions for development of the new suburbs.

Right next to cemetery on acres and acres of land that someday in the future, when it would be needed, could be used for development for additional plots for the cemetery. On that acre and acres of vacant land was a monstrous building sitting way back at the very end of the property. The building was perched on the very top of one of those large rolling hills. It somehow almost resembled a penitentiary. Larger than any other building in that city. It was the town's only orphanage. It stood at least a quarter of a mile from the main road. At night, it had a ghostly image especially under a full moon. And on all Saints Day (Halloween), when the cemetery next to it was all lite up. There were thousands of flickering burning candles that were placed on those graves. The orphanage even appeared to be more of an outlawed place.

Of course, you had to have a large orphanage in that backward town. What could one expect from the uneducated, and those strongly devoted Catholics? They didn't believe in birth control and sex was good for only one thing and that was for was procreation. The Roman Catholic Church considered wasting your seed a mortal sin; therefore, masturbation was a sin. You couldn't even buy prophylactics in Connecticut unless you went to a pharmacist.

The Drug store was the only place that could sell them. It was the law in Connecticut. You could get them, but you had to insist that they were going to be used only in the prevention of disease. Usually with a smile on his face, the pharmacist would sell them to you. In that town, the word, birth-control was never used. Abortion? ______ That word was not even part of their vocabulary.

You needed that orphanage. Yes, there were lots of girls who were under sixteen years of age, unwed mothers, living there with their newly born children.

It was a time when even his ex-wife, as a training nurse, during a delivery, should there be complications, she was told that they must save the child rather than the mother.

"Let the mother die but save the child."

If they didn't obey, those students would be expelled from the hospital and their training as a nurse would be ended.

There was one advantage during this period of time. You didn't have to worry about anyone running off with your child. The orphanage was at its' maximum capacity; even though, it was the largest building in New Britain.

There were few pleasures in that town which consisted of dancing and drinking beer. Dancing was part of their culture. Work hard and then play hard. A few Beers.______Off they went.

From the earliest of years, as a kid, when his grandmother went to a wedding. He noticed that after she had a couple beers, she would get up and do the polka. It would be one dance after another without stopping. It was quite a vigorous dance; something he wouldn't quite master. It was more hopping than dancing.

He also remembered his mother always saying as if it were a great achievement.

"Boy, your uncle is a wonderful dancer. He is so light on his feet."

So, when he danced, he was trying to be light on his feet. It's sort of brought out a different type of energy. The feeling of escaping the pull of gravity.

From this bleak backward background, he saw dancing as an outlet from their boring existence. For a moment, with the sound of a good beat and a good drink, and the use of every muscle in your body, one could escape reality.

That was why dancing was so important to Michael.

Chapter 3

Let The Dancing Begin

They found the table and they ordered their drinks. She ordered her Chardonnay, and he ordered his red wine. After they had a few sips of their drinks, they both watched the dancers on the floor.

With excitement, he turned to Poppy and said. "Let's do it!"

He like his grandmother was one of those dancers that once he got on the Dance Floor; he didn't want to leave. He was surprised how well she kept up with him. She had her own style which was very expressive and suggestive. He was impressed.

They both got in the groove, and they were having a great time. Many more drinks later, they kept dancing. They stayed on the floor until band quit playing. After everyone left, they just sat there.

"I guess it's time to walk you to your car."

When they got there, she had the puzzled look on her face.

"Oh my God, my car is not here!"

By then, of course he knew what had happened. She had parked at the back end of the warehouse and her car was obviously towed. Immediately, he went to the restaurant, and he got the phone number of the towing place. He drove her there to pick up her car. It was a big SUV, and she looked at him, because there was a fine of one hundred and fifty dollars. She didn't have any credit cards with her. He couldn't just leave her there. As a gentleman, he paid to have her car released.

She ran to her car. Overwhelmed with anxiety, the first thing she did was open the glove compartment.

"Oh, it's still there, Thank God!"

With a smile on her face, she pulled out a watch which was covered in diamonds.

"I was so worried that someone would have taken it. I just bought it today and it's worth a lot of money."

From his perspective it looked like junk, costume jewelry.

It was time to say goodbye and he decided to get something for his money. He grabbed her and kissed her. She let him and they did some French kissing. He slowly moved his hand up the front of her dress and caressed her tit and played with her hard nipple. They still were feeling the effect of alcohol, so it wasn't as awkward as someone might think. And she seemed to enjoy his aggressiveness.

As he said goodbye.

"Don't forget you owe me a hundred and fifty dollars."

"I am embarrassed. I will pay you back."

As he drove away, he was thinking that he wasn't particularly interested in seeing her again. He decided to just write off the hundred and fifty dollars. In his mind, it was one of those expensive dates that took a wrong turn.

Chapter 4

Poppy And Shirley

It was the next morning.

"Well, how did your date go?'

It turned out to be a little bit embarrassing. I ended up parked in a shipping area. They towed my car away."

"How did you do something so stupid? Didn't you read the signs? Was it your meds or drinking?"

"I don't know what I was thinking, but I guess I ended up parking behind a loading dock of a warehouse. It was very dark. You know how small the parking areas are in Irvine, just big enough for a compact car. All I know, is I was looking for an area that was wide enough for my SUV."

Almost gasping for air. "It was night, and you know my SUV is so big. I wanted to park it away from the other cars. It was very dark and really it looked like every other parking spot.   I didn't think I needed to worry about something like that at a restaurant. That was my first time there. It was nighttime. Things were slow at the restaurant. I just didn't think parking was going to be problem"

Poppy didn't t mention that there was an announcement.

"I just wasn't paying attention. I was just a little nervous about meeting him."

She sighed. "He had to bail me out by paying for the towing. It cost a hundred and fifty dollars."

"I bet he just loved that. A hundred fifty dollars for the first date, I guess that's going to be the end of that guy?"

"I told him I would pay him back."

"And if he believed you; he is a bigger sucker than I am."

"No, I will pay him back."

Shirley didn't say anything more because she knew Poppy. Poppy was tight with her own money. Although she treated Poppy many times. Poppy never reciprocated, not even once.

"I liked him, and I think we could have fun together. He seemed to be very nice and very open and very giving and a fantastic dancer."

She thought for a while and then said. "Well, if he doesn't call me; I'll call him. He is very different from Joe, and I need something different right now. Joe's kid is getting on my nerves. You know what Tommy said to me the other day."

She tried to mimic a young boy's voice. "You are always in one of your moods. Do you ever smile?"

In her voice of defiance. "Joe has been taking me for granted. He did buy me new tires for my truck. But he bitched at me because he had to do it. Of course, those tires for that SUV aren't cheap. Five hundred dollars each.

But I don't know. I wanted him to take me on a trip to Hawaii but he's so worried about his kid. He wants to take Tommy with us. I don't like being a mother."

Shirley smiled and with a bit of sarcasm. "I need a vacation, too. Don't we all? But my business won't let me."

Now Poppy was angry. "And then after I gave him a great fuck. After he gets what he wants, all he does is sit there and lights up a cigar and smokes it."

Then Shirley nodded her head. "Well, you know what I think of Joe."

"Yeah, I know you don't like him or that he is a cop. You don't have to worry. I will not bring him here to your house. I understand!"

Shirley always on the attack. "By the way, what is going on with your skin? You look like a teenager going through puberty."

"I don't know. I guess; I am going through a bit of stress. You know my sister. She's having a lot of problems."

Shirley shook her head, meaning that she heard that story before.

"You know I have a girlfriend that has similar skin problems. She said that she found this doctor that helped her a lot. He made her change some of the food she was eating, and she said that she has been getting great results. I'll get his phone number for you. Maybe he can help you. Your skin is getting really bad and you need to do something about it."

Poppy's submissive reply. "Okay."

Chapter 5

Let's Hang Out Together

She finally called him a week later.

"Have you forgotten all about me? I though you would call by now. After all, I want to pay you back the money for getting my car out of that place."

He did want to get his hundred and fifty dollars back. He was happy that she called him. He did have a good time with her. He could see where he might be able to have fun with her, but he wasn't infatuated with her. He did feel an attraction for her. She had a nice figure, and she was sexy on that dance floor.

So, he decided to ask her out. He loved Newport and for some reason he was thinking of Mimi's Restaurant. He thought that they might meet at his workplace in Santa Ana sort of a halfway spot, since it was close to Fullerton. She could leave her SUV there, where it would be safe and then he would drive to Newport Beach.

He and Charlie, the Korean owner, were just finishing off a proposal when she arrived. He left her with Charlie while he went to his office to clean off things and this gave Charlie some time to talk with Poppy. Before they left, she needed to go to the rest room. While she was in the restroom, he turned to Charlie to get his opinion. Charlie had a worried and somewhat not approving look on his face.

"She is very hard looking'"

"What does that mean?"

Charlie was loss for words. "Just very hard looking. I like Wendy, better for you."

All the Koreans liked Wendy. Of course, they would; she was very impressed with Koreans and their culture. She knew how to show respect for their culture. They would shower Wendy with expensive significant cultural gifts."

Wendy would say. "They are honoring you, by giving me these gifts."

Wendy was wonderful in so many ways. Mentally, there was something drastically wrong with her. All he knew was there was a part of her almost as if she had multiple personalities. There was one of them that really hated him. Like everything in life our defects stand out more as we age. He imagined that the young Wendy who had the perfect body and face and when she was young, she could wrap almost any man around her figure. She was a German war bride and got pregnant, so the young lieutenant had no choice but to marry her. She ended up getting a Doctorate in Psychology. When he met her, she was in her fifties and still attractive with a body of a lean thirty-year-old weightlifter, with every muscle showing. Being from Europe she loved all foreign cultures.

"I'll see you in the morning Charlie. We can put the finishing touch to that proposal tomorrow."

They were now on their way to Newport Beach. He was disturbed by Charlie's remark. He realized that someone out of his American culture could see something that he himself wouln't be able to see.

As they were walking down the street in Newport Beach on their way to enjoying a meal at Mimi's Restaurant. As soon as they were seated at a table, his mind was on ordering the fabulous onion soup with the thick melted cheese on top and a glass of red wine.

Just then, she turned to him with a whimsical smile on her face and said.

"I'm bisexual."

He wasn't sure why she brought that up. But their conversation, might have been heading towards a relationship. He assumed that it was some sort of flag. Usually, the other person might be trying to tell you that they are or were in a relationship. It was like dating a married woman. You got the cream while the husband got the milk. The husband would have all the daily problems of the relationship while you had all the fun part.

Little further in the conversation she said. "Let's just hang out."

He loved that expression so often used by women under thirty. These younger women didn't want to predict anything, and they just lived for the moment. They were always open to new adventures. No prejudgment, he liked that.

Later he would call Poppy, the Hang Out Girl. Compared to him, she seemed to be so free and open to new experiences.

He had no reference point to what it meant for someone to be bisexual. As a man, a bisexual woman might be a plus. He didn't really weigh in with much of an opinion of her being a bisexual, and what it would mean to their relationship. Why should he, after all it was only their second date. He was rather naive about that kind of sex. He thought that meant a woman won't mind making love to another woman. And that was all there was to it. He had no deeper meaning to what bisexual meant, until much later.

He remembered his son telling him. "God it was unbelievable. I had three women. I never knew that sex could be that good with two women taking care of me while the third women was taking care of them."

Well, he was willing to learn. Maybe he might learn more about that from Poppy. And there was a lot for him to learn. He really wasn't a novice to sex, and he read all the manuals, but they were all limited to having just one woman at a time. And of course, he had a vast collection of X-rated videos. But, after knowing Poppy, they took on whole different meaning. The different fantasies of having three people making love could be unlimited.

When he was younger, he had that boyish clean look. He had been approached by homosexual men. He always found that uncomfortable. Why were they even thinking that he would want to make love to them? Later in life, because of his strong lust for women, it made him wonder if he was compensating for something.

His father had been a very loving man. But, when his father was tossed out by his mother, he felt her pain of being hurt by a man and in this case it, it was his own father. A man, who he also loved and now he also had to cope with his pain of loss. From that pain, disappointment, and his mother's pain, he grew up in not trusting men, and then sometimes mistrusting his own masculinity.

As he progressed through his teens, he learned how to box and adding on his large frame, made him a worthy opponent, most males backed away from a confrontation and those who didn't realized how strong he was. They backed away almost immediately. He found that most men were bullies. He also learned to compete using his intellect and strategy. He saw men as the weaker sex and very monodirectional. Males seemed more interested in conquest, whereas females were interested in feelings. They were sensual creatures like his cat. They were into softness and delicate touching.

When he said he wasn't interested in nice way as not to hurt their feelings. Some of these men would persist in a sort of clever way. He thought that they thought he was giving off some kind vibe. Maybe they saw something that he didn't see. He never felt comfortable with other boys or men. He always looked at them as competition. He had never liked the swaggering posturing of the male animal.

In general, he didn't feel comfortable with men. He always felt that he had to compete with them. He couldn't feel any tenderness toward a male until he had his son. When his son was growing up, they kissed in public until his son reached a certain age. It was very healing process for him in having a son. As he matured, he became tolerant of other males.

Chapter 6

The City Of Orange

Today, they were to meet in the City of Orange. In the past, he paid little attention to the beauty of the city. Even though, Michael had driven so many times up and down those streets. It could have been the place of where he grew up. Orange was quaint city with buildings that looked like they might have been in New England. The main street where they were to meet was on a Round About. The Round About was rare for California but so common back on the East Coast. He had known of only two other intersections of that type in Southern California. One was in Long Beach, and another was in La Quinta. It was fun driving around and around on them and it felt dangerous. It felt like you were caught in a centrifugal force and when you were ready you could peel off zinging as if released from sling shot, following a straight line, off onto your destination.

Every time he flashed around this circle in Orange; he thought of his childhood in Connecticut. His Sunday afternoon ride in his grandfather's nineteen thirty-seven Hudson's, a black roomy coach like structure. It could have been a room in someone's home, padded in expensive leather. Today, no one would even know the name of those classic cars, Hudson, Packard, or Nash. It brought back those feelings, their ritualistic Sunday drive. It was traditional for people to tour in their automobiles on Sunday and they all congregated into the center of downtown.

He could remember that moment with his grandfather, as if it were frozen in time. Just the thought of that precious moment made him cry. He was only four years old, but he could feel the pride that his grandfather felt to have him sitting next to him in that big airy Hudson, his first and only American grandson.

He remembered how his grandfather had a tool that he used to clip one end of a cigar. He smelled the robust aroma of the cigar. His grandfather would lick the end of the cigar. How that end glistened in the afternoon's Connecticut humid air. He would strike a large match. Now his grandfather moved the cigar through the air as if to show it off. With the flame from the match, he held it next to the end and sucked until there was a glow coming from the end of the cigar and now the smoke and the strong aroma of that smoke filled the interior of the car. He loved that smell and every time he smelled it, as he did now, it was a reminder for Michael why his grandfather died early in life because of that vicious habit.

On their way to downtown, they would have to past through the site of many tall buildings that were on each side of them. He knew they were called factories. That day, there wasn't any pounding noises, because it was Sunday, and no one worked on Sunday. To a child, downtown was special because he could see through all the large glass windows of all the stores, and their display of beautiful objects. Also, there were a multitude of tracks as the trolleys moved back and forth ringing and clanging of bells and their beautiful sounds. It was very exciting. They didn't travel far before they hit the large circle, much larger than the one in Orange. This large circle surrounded a small park, an island with monuments to the heroes of past, veterans of the Civil War. Later in his life, this place became important place because of the convenience of a wonderful underground rest room, open day, and night.

Now, he was back in Orange, and he had driven through this circle. He realized that he was excited to be meeting with Poppy.

Chapter 7

Shopping with Poppy

They agreed to meet on Main Street under the big clock, at four o'clock sharp. There wouldn't be any excuse about the time, not while there was this large clock on streetlight like pole above him and just glaring down on him. He watched as the cars whizzed around and around the circle. As always, he was early, and the street were disserted. So, when she approached, he would not have any trouble spotting her from far away.

The area had a little college atmosphere to it. It was only a few blocks away from Chapman College. Poppy seemed attracted to these little cities. Fullerton had the same flavor. She liked shops and she liked quaint little restaurants. In their history together, they would spend many hours going up and down the streets of Fullerton. It was reminiscent of his many walks with his mother, shopping here and there. As a little boy, it was rather boring going in and out of stores or for him to sit while his mother tried on a new dress.

His mother would have to constantly scold him with reminders. "Someday, women will recognize the good training, I am giving you."

As she was walking down the street, his unfocused vision could not distinguish who she was. Even at the very moment, when she walked up to him and greeted him, he wasn't sure that he recognized her. She had on a long fully masking black trench coat (black was always her favorite color). The kind of coat that Dracula or the Shadow would wear.

She exuded a boyish appearance. Her black kinky curly hair covered part of her face and she radiated a plain and maybe even a hard look of a teenage boy. As always, she wore no makeup, and her lips were covered with a glistening colorless lipstick. She embraced him and snuggled in; he was overwhelmed by a strong attracting force. He could feel her warmth. He knew he wore a defensive armor and was emotionally distanced. Yet with her, right at this moment, he felt her radiation and fondness for him, and he felt her body melting into his. He just didn't feel that way with many women.

She was there with him, and she was going to take him for a tour. All he could do was follow her as she took him in and out of every little shop. He was amazed and impressed to see all those antiques and collector items. It was like eBay but contained in real shops. He was fascinated seeing collections of coin operated commercial record playing machine, juke boxes and their very various colorful lite displays that would make them stand out in the good old days. He was also fascinated by the assortment of pin ball machines, something he could never get enough of as a kid.

Boy, could she shop. She would pensively stop and look as if pondering a major decision. She would touch the object and then walk around it. Slowly, she would study it looking at it from top to bottom and touch it again and then finally walk on to the next display.

Why did she go through this stupid ritual? For one, he could follow that she liked doing it and she had knack of finding objects that she could sell for lot more than what she paid for them. She always had a certain taste for good collectibles. She was amazing in so many different ways. He never seemed to tire of her doing her little dance. He would look at her face and posture when she saw something she liked. She would look like a little girl who discovered something wonderful (like looking at a butterfly when you are young). Suddenly, her color changed, and her facial expressions changed. And then, as she walked away, there was an expression of disappointment.

Just before leaving the store. She would go back to the object that she spent most of her time with. It was a very quick glace backwards, followed by her brisk walk, moving away. And as he looked at her, she seemed to have had smile on her face. Then, her nonplussed standard face appeared.

Chapter 8

Billiard With A Twist

He had no idea how they ended at a pool hall. It was something she wanted to do. I guess it was time to take a break and have beer and something to do to whittle away the time. It was a strange pool hall but than what did he know, he wasn't a pool hall fan. Poolrooms never attracted the best people, so he thought, but this place was bare and had nothing like the upbeat pool halls near Cal State Fullerton. He preferred the classy places, but she always found those little dives. She liked mystery and a place where no one would know her, and this was that place. It seemed a little run down but again he had learned she liked that. And being with her, he liked it, too. He thought if he were back in Connecticut, their pool halls might look like this old place. Places that had been around for a least a hundred years.

He wasn't any good at pool, but what could he do but humor her. This world was so foreign to him. He knew why she liked pool. He saw her play many times. She looked like a champion when she played. She was a celebrity in that kind of environment. It was an open place where men acted aggressively toward women. It was equal to a woman being in an all-male locker room. He had learned that she knew where to go to be picked up. This pool hall was a man's hangout.

She had told him about her many different experiences.

"When I am depressed, I would end up at a place like this, where big rigs drivers hang out."

It wasn't the kind of people, he associated with.

Chapter 9

The Enchanted Cottage

His mother was a movie enthusiast and so in the forties; she would take him with her as her escort. He would be forced to see all those romantic black and white classics with her. Throughout his life, he would have flashbacks to flicker from those precious childhood years. They were framed in the naïve thoughts of a younger mind. One movie played over in his head. It was a story of two disfigured lovers, who lived in their enchanted cottage. Their faces disfigured from flesh that had been burned. From the thoughts in a child's brain, he would never see anyone so horribly disfigured. Yet these people were able to see themselves as beautiful people without their ugly scars. They both felt beautiful but only they could see that beauty and no one else could. All his life, he envied those two lovers. What a wonderful, enchanted cottage that was.

Yet, when he was with Poppy, he felt he had entered this enchanted cottage and he knew that she had the power to do that with him, and to anyone she wished to do that to. Could she continue using this power of her illusion, over him as well as other people? He learned that she could. It was all dependent on how long you kept her interest. When she got bored, she dropped you like a hot potato and she never looked back.

Love what was that? He heard those words over and again. "Don't you want someone to love you?" Of course, he wanted to be loved. Didn't everyone?

But what was love. It was some illusion. A moment in that enchanted cottage. It never lasted long. Even when someone loved him, he could feel himself changing. He then changed so much that he fell out of love, or they fell out of love with him. I guess that was the perspective, the Gestalt of it.

Yet why did those feelings for his cat last so long? Did you love an animal? Could a human feel love toward an animal? Was that love? It felt like love. There was a bonding, certain expectation of affection from another living creature.

How do you define love? He wanted to put it into a category in the same way you define things in biology. What made something living? For one, it was ability to reproduce. He understood reproduction from an early age. As a child who couldn't play with other children because his mother didn't tolerate him getting dirty. Which wasn't too ridiculous for that day and age? Laundering was difficult. Baths where still an inconvenience. Bathrooms, showers and hot water weren't part of the household. Their house was built in the early part of the nineteen hundred and there was poor heating of water for a bath. There was a heater in a closet that used gas. One would feed it quarters as one did with a meter. Someone from the gas company would come around once a month and empty it.

So, because of that restriction on playing, he led a solitary life and spent time entertaining himself. He loved looking through a microscope and seeing one cell creatures eating, moving, and dividing. Dividing in minutes and producing matching reproductions of themselves. How many hours did he spend studying them? As he studied these creatures, they almost had a personality. Some had little flashing cilia that moved them to food or away from a bright light.

Later he realized that blood cells as well as viruses also reproduced. He had learned that he was a mammal, warm blooded, had hair or fur, breast-feed their young and enjoyed touching. Like all mammals because of their caring from their mother there was a closeness to their mother. He also liked touching and the warmth of another body and the breathing and the sound of a heart beating. There were certain contracts that one performed with another living creature, feeding, cleaning. He would watch his unicellular creatures die because their own waste would eventually kill them; however, if he changed the water and balanced the food intake they would multiply forever.

When Mary Queen of the Scotts was beheaded, her dog stopped eating and eventually died. Yes, in true love there was that feeling that you could die for that other creature.

Vacuuming and cleaning up after the creature. There were even moments of accidents, inconvenience or when the creature was bothersome. When he wanted attention from you, and you weren't ready or when you were busy or tired. There were disturbing noises in the middle of the night because he was a night creature, or he heard something that your human ears couldn't hear. Yet the bond between, the two, seemed consistent. Would he still love this creature, if Mambo didn't show him any affection and would Mambo show him affection if he didn't feed him and take care of him?

Wasn't that what he had learned in biology? Symbiosis is parasitic relationship where two creatures need each other for their existence; the bacterium in our gut is a good example. The old symbiotic relationships, the general give and take. Parasitic, in human relationships, disguised as give and take. Some men just wanted their mother. Michael just wanted sex and most importantly someone who could hold his attention.

When he explained all of this to Poppy, she was in full agreement. She had been used and used people for too many years not to confirm his argument. Yet the society he lived-in refused to shed their illusions. Most would hide behind their religious beliefs and talk about the sanctity of marriage. His society had not progressed much from the time of Thomas Harding when one of his books was ban because he wrote something about divorce. Love was supposedly a sacrament. He saw love as a symbiotic relationship. One had to learn how to keep the illusions going to keep it exciting and rewarding. Oh, the work part of the relationship could keep people going and staying together but you needed more to keep those juices going. His cat won't be part of warm and caring relationship, if he constantly interfered with his life. Yet he had far too many relationships where the demand of one's partner would become excessive and whatever rewards that were left; they weren't worthwhile to keep the whole thing going. Marriage was like so many commission jobs. Positions where you were led by a carrot believing that you were going to make five thousand dollars a month. Only exceptional people did that. Wasn't marriage and relationships something like that?

Poppy knew how to hold his interest. They would have their many crescendos of an exciting sex together. She was intriguing. She was well-read and continued to have many friendships apart form their own. He found that stimulating and he liked it. He surprised himself in that in the beginning he wasn't jealous. When she was with him, she made him feel like he was the only real person in her life.

Yet, she with her triple standards wanted him all to herself. He didn't need any other woman. Even when she wasn't with him, he could think of her. Whatever she gave him. It was like a battery and that he could store and charge it. Of course, like any battery she would recharge him. This was her uniqueness. She gave him so much when she was with him that he didn't need to see her for a week or two. She also sensed how long that period would be, and she was always there when he would need the next recharge. Sometimes, it would be like today, just spending time playing pool.

There was a kind of tranquility that she gave him; yet, in those same moments, he knew there was tranquility that he gave her. They both lived hectic and confused lives. They lived-in a society that demanded a lot from them and these moments together were soothing for both. Love, he thought also included moments where two creatures ran smoothly, like a well-tuned car.

He looked around the room to see if any of the other men were looking at her. He noticed that none of the other men or other faces even looked at her. This was so unusual, since she was the only woman in the whole pool hall. He was watching, and he didn't even see a quick look, not even a side glance of the eye.

He didn't understand his emotions. He was used to being with beautiful women and yet she was so ugly that none of the men even looked at her. Inside of himself, he felt good, no one wanted her but himself. He felt love for her and as if he was holding the secret that she was beautiful. He would be the only one who could see her as being beautiful, like in the enchanted cottage. He didn't understand that feeling but nevertheless it was there. It was like he was on his own private island, and he made up all the rules. And she was the most attractive woman in the whole wide world. But there was something more, a titillating feeling. She had that unisex mode, being neither a man nor a woman.

She jester to him and then said. "I need to go to the rest room."

He wanted to be naughty. "Why don't you take off all your clothes while you are there and wear only that coat of yours. I know you want to play pool maybe you can give the guys something to look at while you are playing".

Chapter 10

The Shot

When she came back, he opened the bottom part of her coat, just enough so her pubic area would be visible. She didn't shave down there. He did shave her once, but she didn't like it so that all her pubic hair had grown back. He wondered would those men notice her. Would they look at her and desire her the same way he did. He wanted everyone there to fuck her yet knowing that she belonged to him and that he owned her. That she belonged to him and only him.

Or would they just feel sorry for him for being with such a homely woman? Did they think that maybe she was in fact one of them, a male? Caught back by his thoughts, he was thinking of her in those terms. He studied her and like being hit by a cold Pacific Ocean spray, he saw her looking that way. Was she a boy or a woman? She liked doing that to him. She enjoyed looking like a boy and being a boy. He felt that she wanted to show him; she wanted him to know that she could get him to like her in any way she wished, as a boy, or as a woman.

She wanted him to understand what kind of power she had over him. She possessed energy. With the message that everything goes. Yes, when she wished it, she would have all eyes on her.

Subconsciously, from deep within him something gushed to the surface. She wanted to be with him, today. He had her all to himself. His body now flushed with that power of his singular possession of her. Was he in love with her and was she in love with him? It sure felt like that.

She was leaning over the pool table with her black trench coat. The bottom part of the trench coat opened enough to give a hint of what was underneath. She lined up her shot. She went down into crouch and from that position she jumped up into the air. While connecting that motion into a lethal jab with her cue stick and hitting the ball with a force that was equivalent of an atomic blast. And now, the ball she hit leaped forward at the other balls that she needed to play. He heard a vicious crack as it hit the targeted ball. Her act of hitting balls looked more like something performed by a ballerina. It was beautiful and he knew what to look for as her trench coat opened for just a split second.

Well, that kind of shooting got the crowds' attention. Suddenly, the table was surrounded by players. Bets were going every which way and there was a percentage for her. The crowd got bigger, and the bids got higher. She milked the spectators. The game went on. She did well until the last rounds. She finally smiled, backed off and took her money.

As they walked out of the place, and they were outside. She whispered to Michael, "I am better than that. I was a bit rusty; I haven't played for some time."

Then with a smile. "But your trench coat idea did give me some advantages."

Her pockets were stuffed with all kinds of bills. She finally pulled all the bills together. She paused counting each bill and then slid the roll of bills deep inside of her trench coat. She was happy.

Chapter 11

Getting ready for Tucson

She walked in right on time, and she had a gift in her hand it was for his birthday. It was exquisitely wrapped and looked as if a professional had wrapped it.

"Boy, that wrapping looks beautiful did you do that by yourself?"

She smiled. "Yes, I did. It's just something I like to do."

He felt the wrapping of a gift should be honored. He hated it when his grandkids would just tear off the paper without paying any attention to how it was wrapped. As he opened the package, he was very careful not to destroy the wrapping. In fact, over time he would have many of these wrappings and he would hang them up in the garage. In his garage was a fully equipped gym, and he spent a lot of time there. He would admire those wrappings, their beauty, and the way they were put together. The ribbons were bowed into perfect looking flowers. The color and the ribbons and everything about the wrapping were unique. It had to take a lot of time to make them look so beautiful.

She liked buying him books and this time it was a set of four books on different sexual stories. It was a special collection that he would later honor in his life and read over and over. She always honored him with special gifts like that.

He wasn't ready to go. He was in the process of making a tuna fish sandwich for the trip. She saw everything laid out in the kitchen. She spoke. "Well let me do that and you go ahead and finish up and get ready for us to go."

He watched her as she took over and daintily cut the onions and celery and found the mayonnaise in the refrigerator, found the bread, and found aluminum foil. When he came back, she had all the sandwiches wrapped neatly in tin foil and in a plastic bag ready to go. Now, they were on their way.

Michael decided that since he had traveled to Arizona and Tucson so many times on business, that he wanted to take the lower route through San Diego. He thought it was more picturesque and straightforward rather than the passage through Blythe and Phoenix.

They finally hit the rest stop that was high up in the mountains halfway to Tucson but still in California. He decided to sit down and have one of the sandwiches and they were delicious. She waved him off that she wasn't interested eating. When they were ready to go, there was a slight snow flurry, and they were worried that the roads might get snowed in. Before they left, he couldn't help admiring little flurries of light snowflakes as they lay on her black hair and slowly dissolving. For some reason, it made him feel romantic. He had to lean over and give her a big kiss and she seemed to be receptive. It was just one of those magical moments.

When they got to the car. He was a little nervous because he had not driven in the snow for a long time and although there wasn't a lot of snow on the road; it could be dangerous. I guess she saw his nervousness.

She said. "I like to drive and I'm tired of just sitting and I'm a good driver. I've driven ten wheelers and limousines before."

He was more than happy to let her drive. She didn't disappoint him; she was a great driver and he noticed that a few times the car slid but she caught it.

It was still a long drive from there to Tucson. When they arrived, the sun was setting, and it was quickly getting dark. He wanted to get a room that had a jacuzzi in it. He loved using the jacuzzi and Valerie thought him how to use it to improve their love making. They found a motel that did have the jacuzzi. Now that they had their room, they decided that they would grab something to eat in the kitchen that was part of the motel. The kitchen was almost closed, and they were their last customers. He got a hamburger something that was easy for the restaurant to make. She got a cheese sandwich but they both wanted something to drink for him it would be wine, and she wanted a Bloody Mary. She got her Bloody Mary, but she wanted more of the condiments. She liked her Bloody Mary hot, lots of Tabasco sauce. He saw that the waitress was tired and asked if he could go in the kitchen and get some Tabasco sauce. Poppy was so impressed, that he went out of his way, just to accommodate her. By now they were not feeling any pain. He had grown a lot of marijuana in his little garden, so he had plenty. When they got back, and he fixed a pipe and lit it up got a good hit and then kissed her. He blew it into her, and they did this for a while, and she got comfortable just lying in the jacuzzi. They did that for at least a couple of hours until they were exhausted. She enjoyed the water as much as he did. She was a Pisces. She would tell him later that it was the perfect thing that he did with the marijuana and the jacuzzi. It was exactly what her body needed.

Chapter 12

They Could Move To Tucson

It was a new day and the first thing on their agenda was to find out whether Poppy could transfer from St Jude Hospital in Fullerton to Saint Mary's Hospital in Tucson. They were sister hospitals and there was good possibility that she might be able to do that. He was waiting in the car while she went up to talk to Human Resources.

While he waited, he got on his mobile phone to check to see if he could line himself up with a realtor. The plan was to look at different properties in Tucson and get sort of fix on what it would cost and to get idea of what was available. To see if anything would turn them on and make them want to move.

It wasn't too long before she was bouncing down the stairs of the hospital with a smile on her face. Well, that was surprisingly good sign.

"You know they told me that I can keep all my benefits, retirement, and everything in my transfer here."

She was full of pride when she said. "They'd be more than happy to hire me right now."

"That is great news and while you were in the hospital; I was on the phone, and I contacted a realtor. Gave him a sort of ballpark figure and price range. He said he had about three or four different places for us to look at right now."

They took off to the realtor's office. They went through the typical introduction. They jumped into the realtor's large SUV, and they were off. The first place that he took them turned out to be a rather interesting site and it was dirt cheap. It was a mobile home that was firmly anchored to a concrete slab on sort of the hill that overlooked a road that bordered on a State Preserve. The view was breathtaking sight of many Saguaro Cactuses and lots of open space ending with a backdrop of mountains. The lot was large over two and a half acres. That is a lot of land for a Californian. They both noticed that most of the neighbors had horses which was a good sign.

But once they got inside of the place; it was obvious why the deal was so reasonable. Just about everything inside needed to be gutted. The kitchen was bad, and the windows weren't big enough. It was dingy inside the place plus the air conditioning didn't seem to be working very well. It was a major Fixer-Upper however the price was very reasonable especially with 2 and ½ acres of land.

Of course, the realtor wasn't stupid. He couldn't help noticing their disappointment. They did see some other places and were genuinely nice but none of them had the scenery that the old run-down modular home had.

They left the realtor with the thought that they had to think about it, but they did like the first place with the great view except they didn't quite understand what to do with the inside of the place. They couldn't resist but to go back to that place and take another look at it by themselves.

Poppy's comment, "Well it sort of looks like us great on the outside but like us pretty shitty on the inside."

He wasn't quite sure what she meant by that, but he knew that she felt that her insides were always a medical problem, and he did complain a lot about his frequent urinary tract infections.

He decided that he wanted to talk to some of the neighbors. She went along with the plan, and they walked to the nearest neighbor who had two or three horses. Seeing the horses, he saw that as a good premonition. The night before he a dream about horses and he was a believer of visions.

Michael introduced himself. "You know we're looking at that place over there. Just wondering if you know any history or anything about it?"

"It's been empty for a while. I don't know very much about it. The people who lived there weren't very neighborly. It was an older couple and I guess his wife passed on and he moved somewhere else."

Kinney was a contractor and when Michael learned that he said.

"You know that inside of that place really needs a lot of fixing up. Is that something that you might be able to do? The kitchen is just awful, and I think that air conditioner needs to be replaced. I live in Huntington Beach, but in the meantime, if I did purchase the home; I would probably have someone work on it. Clean it up inside before we even moved in. It's not livable the way it is. Is that something that you could do? You can take your time and be close to where you live. You can work on it sort of piecemeal. It's not something that has to be done overnight.

"I'm always looking for work being a contractor. Yes, it's something that I do and can do well. The kitchen certainly needs to be refurbished and the windows need to be changed.   I know it has a great view of The Preserve. That is one of the things I like about living here and it's even better on horseback. The best thing about this place, there isn't any traffic on that road. It's quiet and peaceful."

The more Poppy and Michael talked about the place; the more excited they seem to get. As soon as Michael got up in the next morning, he called the realtor. The realtor said that for financial reasons, he could get waiver on that the property which would make the financing with the bank easier. It would be considered a summer home. Michael could keep his place in Huntington Beach and wouldn't be any problem with the bank. In the meantime, he needed to get their social security numbers from both and other credit information so he could get the ball rolling.

He turned to Poppy. "I need your social security number."

Poppy turned rigid and a blank expression came over her face.

"I'm sorry, I just can't do that."

Although Michael could have done the deal on his own credit, he noticed that the agents voice sounded strange and different when he heard the bad news.

He had noticed that the realtor didn't seem to take a liking to Poppy when they first met.   Michael could understand that because Poppy did look young, and her face was blooming with a bad case of acne.

"Okay, let's see what you can do with my credit alone."

At this point, Michael was surprised and disappointed with Poppy. He was smart enough to know something was wrong and he decided not to discuss it any further with her. Anyways, it was time for lunch, and maybe she would say something at lunch.

At the restaurant, as he looked through the menu, he peeked over the top of the sheet to see her face. Her facial expression hadn't changed. There was just this blank look on her face without any kind of expression. He knew something was going on; she wasn't ready to tell him what she was thinking. He realized that he couldn't pull the deal off without her cooperation.

When he was alone, he called the realtor. "No, I don't think we're going to be able to swing the deal. She doesn't seem to want to give me her social security. I really like that place and I know that if I got it fixed up it would be great, but at this point, I'm going to have to drop out of the deal without her help. It's just not going to work."

He noticed the realtor didn't react the way he had expected. Instead, he reacted as if he knew that this was going to happen. I guess as a realtor you get to see a lot of looky-loos.

Chapter 13

Coming Clean

Nothing much more was said. It was about four o'clock, and they were now at a local restaurant and getting ready to return to Huntington Beach. He tried to get her to talk some more, but she wasn't saying anything. He fed her a couple a Bloody Mary's

"I was married to someone when I was twenty-eight. I ended up in the hospital with this problem. They told me that part of my small intestine was almost dissolved, eaten away. They had to operate and remove it and I had a colostomy, for just a short time, while they were waiting for the area to heal. I spent a lot of time in a hospital and Walter, who was sort of a friend, visited me all the time. He was there for me every day. He was so caring, and he brought me magazines, flowers, and all kinds of little gifts. He cheered me up. He finally asked me to marry him, and my mother was very encouraging. She thought being married would be good for me. I could give up being a prostitute or being in that lifestyle. Walter and I had a good life. He was a contractor and made good money. We had a beautiful home with everything that I would ever want.

I know Walter was abused by his uncle in his childhood, but I never thought anything more about it except that he might be bi. I really didn't think it was a big thing, but then he got involved in all these different groups of people in the gay community. He even was part of the gay parade."

She showed her disgusted look. Michael also knew that she could be very private about her sexuality and did not consider herself to be lesbian.

"Yeah, I can accept that I'm bisexual, but I don't want to advertise it to everyone. Walter ended up in jail for two years for dealing and possession of marijuana. I didn't want any part of that, so we got divorced."

She laughed. "Actually, I just ran into him the other day at the supermarket. I don't feel anything for him, and I even wondered why I ever married him. Oh, this is the funny part; he introduced me to his new girlfriend. She was beautiful. I was in fact jealous; I could have gone down on her easily. I wouldn't have guessed it until he told me. She was a transvestite. He was excited; he wanted to introduce her to his family. I don't think he was going to tell them that she was a transvestite. In a way, I felt sorry for him and another way I felt happy for him, but I was happy that he was out of my life."

She was on a roll. She would tell him how she met Nick and she ended in one of her grand adventures. He would later hear that story many times, and never got tired of hearing her story. She financed a truck with him and got conned into becoming a cosigner on a new rig. He took off and left her with the payments.

But as she told the story repeatedly, it took on a different color each time. "A little later I meant Nick who was much older than me, but he owned a truck one of those ten-wheeler and we went on trips together. It was a lot of fun traveling in one of those babies and you have a cabin on the upside with a bed and everything. We fucked in there a lot. I fell in love with him. He reminded me of my father. He wanted me to go in with him to buy a new truck.

He said he could make a lot more money using it and that we could be joint business partners and so I signed my name as part of the loan documents.

Because of his workload and my shifts, I wouldn't see him for weeks. I became suspicious, so I hired a private eye. All the private eye told me is that I shouldn't want any part of him and that he had a wife and several girl friends in different states. I said my goodbye to him, by giving him one last good fuck that he could never forget."

Michael knew how she could do that because she would do it to him in her loving way. She was full of power and vigor, one thing Poppy never lacked was energy. With this guy, like all her addictions, she went cold turkey and never saw him again. He understood what she experienced, and it was all so typical of so many of us, including his own adventures. We pick on people who are unavailable because we ourselves are unavailable. He could only assume that this kind of hang-up came from early childhood feelings of abandonment.

"I was pretty pissed off and I also was depressed. I decided to hang out at this bar where a lot of truckers stop over. I had one too many drinks and what I didn't know was that the cops use that place to get their quotas. I was a dead giveaway because when I took off, I remember hearing the noise of the pebbles flying. They got me dead on for DUI. I had to spend thousands of dollars plus take one of those courses every week that's how I met Joe; he was one of the instructors of the class. I even commented to Shirley whether I should start up with this guy or not? I knew he liked me because he was hitting on me. He kept asking me out and I finally gave in. I sort of liked him and he was a cop, and he was willing to spend money on me. He is very generous. I was a little suspicious of him because his wife committed suicide by jumping off the top of their house and left her son behind."

She sighed. "So that brings you pretty much up-to-date and now you know why I didn't want to give you my social security number."

He looked at her and spoke. "Well, if you've got this thing going with Joe, why were you doing the dating game?"

"Well, I think it's obvious. I'm not happy with Joe and I don't know if I want to be a mother to a young boy, after his mother had committed suicide. What kind of woman would do that? There must have been something bad between Joe and her."

Since they had agreed that their relationship would be loose and easy and just sort of hanging out together, he had no reason to be jealous or in a position to have any kind of possessive feelings. He felt the most important thing at this time was that they should be having fun together. Why not enjoy what he had. In her mind, she also felt that he was attached and still involved with Wendy.

After finishing the second drink she pretty much passed out. He got her into the car, but she just slumped into unconsciousness. The weather had gotten mean, and it was raining, and the roads that he was taking were secondary and quite far from the main highway. He was struggling with his driving until he could get to a major highway.

They were now in Yuma, California. Poppy finally awoke from her deep slumber that knocked her out after her two Bloody Mary's.

"Well, you missed the worst part of the driving. It was raining and there were lots of cars."

She saw that he was exhausted and so she offered to drive. "You look tired, and I am rested. That nap did me a lot of good. Would you like me to drive?"

He saw that she was sober, and he decided to let her drive "Yeah, I'm pretty tired and there's a gas station up ahead and I need to gas up so we can switch out there."

Letting a woman drive was never an issue. Her didn't have to play, The Macho Guy.

People told him. "You drive like an old lady."

He had to drive his grandmother around town. She wasn't accustomed to riding in a car, so he had to be gentle in taking corners and stopping. Of course, New Britain, Connecticut had old roads designed more for horses than cars. It was hilly and the speed limit was mostly twenty -five mile and hour. It was uncommon for women to drive when he was growing up. His mother was a unique woman. Not only was she beautiful, but she was always well-groomed and had a little bit of discipline or elitism. At the time, he was growing up very few women drove; in fact, there were very few cars on the road. He always had a favorite picture to show people, streets bare of automobiles. No cars going up and down the streets. In fact, people still used horses. He could remember the Milkman, horse and wagon and delivering milk to each one of the residents. There was even, the Iceman in his horse and truck wagon delivering huge ice blocks. They didn't have refrigeration; they only had ice boxes.

His mother was unusual in that she was a single woman in a town that was very Catholic. She was divorced but she always looked quite beautiful always in a beautiful dress, well made up. She dressed so well that he assumed for that low-class town that a lot of people thought she was a prostitute. His mother and one other woman were the only females that he ever saw driving besides some teachers. The other woman drove a big Packard. She and her husband own a very prominent gas station. Her son, Paul, had paralysis from polio and Michael was his only friend and was always offered a ride from school.

Poppy got behind the wheel and got going on the freeway. She hit speeds in his car that he didn't quite know that it would go that high and drive that well, after all it was only a Toyota Corolla. She said that she was quite aware of what she was doing, and he was confident that they would not be pulled over for speeding because she was looking all over the place. He had a sense that if there were any police in the area; she would spot them.

"Where did you learn to drive this well?"

"Oh, when I was living with my girlfriend, I decided to become a limousine driver. It's pretty much like driving a regular car just a little longer."

She was being very talkative, which meant that she was relaxed with him, and she was beginning to trust him.

"You know when I got to Vegas, I was only fourteen years old, but I had some guy that was looking out for me. He set me up in business with a high-class clientele and fortunately for me I never had to work the streets. I finally met some guy that was doing very well. He was a professional gambler. He gave me everything I ever wanted in terms of money. He took particularly good care of me in fact I have his last name." He didn't know if that meant that she had married him, but he assumed that she had been and just wasn't telling him that.

"I fell in love with this beautiful young thing. I had to give up what I did before, and I decided that I would do the limousine work to pay for our relationship. She was young and beautiful, and I couldn't resist. Being in the limousine business, I kept up with some contacts and made new contacts. I had got lots invites to parties, but I couldn't make it to one of them, so I sent her to the party. The feedback I got was that she was very inappropriate or immature and drank too much. One of my friends said. "I can't believe that you're associated with that thing.""

Frank was pretty upset with me for leaving him for a woman. He called my mother. My Mother called me. "What are you thinking? How could you love a woman? You had it made with that rich guy taking care of you."

"My answer was that if you haven't tried it than don't complain."

Michael found conversation fascinating and she just kept talking. Going over ninety miles an hour, before they knew it. They were back at his place. By now, she looked tired and so he fixed her a meal and gave her a Xanax to relax her. He tucked her in bed and very quickly she was asleep.

In the morning, when she woke up, looking very refreshed. She thanked him for his patience and that he took such good care of her. He never again mentioned anything about the house in Tucson.

"Thank you so much for such a good time I really needed that and especially the jacuzzi and the marijuana."

They kissed and she left, but when she got home, she couldn't stop talking to Shirley about what a wonderful time she had and how much she liked him.

Chapter 14

His Walk On The Beach

It was a Wednesday afternoon around 12:30. After grabbing some food, he felt good and decided to take the afternoon off. It was not an ideal day for the beach. The fog had lifted but the sun was still obscured, by a thick cloud cover. He decided to take the bike rather than walking because with the bike; he was just minutes away from the ocean.

When he first came to Huntington Beach in 1965, he and his family visited the pier on a Saturday. There was no one there and that validated his difficult move from the East Coast. It was so different from Jones Beach in New York. How many Saturdays or Sundays had they had gone to Jones Beach, one of those cities' beaches and by the time they got there at 9AM, it was already too late. Jones was filled to its' capacity. Even if you got there early the beach was no longer a beach but just blankets next to blankets. As you tried to get near the water, you couldn't help but walk on someone's blanket.

One reason he came to California, it was that no one owned the beach, whereas back East the beaches were owned by individuals. You couldn't do what he was about to do. The only real dissatisfaction was that the Pacific Ocean was a lot colder than the Atlantic, that disappointed him.

In a blink of an eye, he was looking at an unlimited horizon. He experienced his two favorite things about the beach, the smell of the fresh salt air without smog, and the rhythmic pounding of water against the shore. It was there today, and he wasn't disappointed. Now that he was there, to his surprise there wasn't a soul on the beach. It had to be the overcast that kept people away. Because the rays of the sun were blocked by the upper fog, the scenery looked as if someone was shooting a movie in black and white instead of color. Everything looked grayish in color, the sand, the water, the sky.

Since he had the beach all to himself, he would go right down into the surf. He wanted to be right up there on the edge, where the water rolled up to the dry sand. He tried to ride on the sand. If he stayed on the edge, where the water met with the dry sand, the surface would be hard enough for the tires to have traction that he needed. He was able to maneuver just above the surf as it rolled in.

The tires created a sort of squishing sound against his sand road and the front of the bike created a pattern in the sand as it moved over it, pushing the water out. Watching those patterns was hypnotic, putting him into a meditative mood. What impressed him the most was how quickly he could transverse the area on his bike as opposed to having to walk that distance. He decided to go from east to west, as far as Warner. That area would be right up to where Huntington Beach met Seal Beach; he estimated that would be about five miles of beach.

He was having a ball getting the tires into the water just enough so that they were not submerged, and he was able to pedal as if he was on a dry creek concrete road. He biked for about a mile, and it was wonderful to hear the roar of the waves coming in. Peddling along, he saw no cars, no people and just the sound of the ocean.

He came up to a flock of a hundred or more pelicans on the shores end and many baby pelicans. As he approached, they all took off going into the west and away from him all flying in counter-clock pattern. They would circle all the way around and came back from the east and then they landed one by one. He decided to move about twenty feet up on the sand, on a little hill of sand. He just sat and watched them. Some of them flew out into the ocean and then took a dive and obviously caught a fish or something and brought it back to the group. Occasionally, they would hear an imagined noise or distraction and they would all flutter off. But then they would circle around and, in their hundreds, come back. he must have sat there for more than an hour just watching them.

The Pelicans were very interesting looking with their large beaks and the pouch that projected underneath those large beaks. They looked somewhat like a prehistoric creature not sleek so true of our present time. They looked so ungraceful on land and yet once airborne appeared to be so majestic with their large wingspan. He felt that looking at them was so entertaining and always in way in the background were the pelicans flying and then zooming down to catch something in the ocean and then flying, up and away again

He had to smile in the way the pelican would wobble so ungracefully before take-off. He couldn't help but smile. Once they were airborne, they were so graceful the way they flowed with the wind. He shouldn't have been surprised in seeing so many pelicans. He knew that on the other side of Pacific Coast Highway to the north was a bird preserve. It was a lagoon, where birds migrated from all over the world.

Today it was a little chilly and he had appropriate clothes, pants, shoes and sweater and he was comfortable. But he was getting hungry, and he was thinking about the Jack in the Box that was on the corner of Warner and Pacific Coast Highway. He wanted to get there and have a Diet Coke and a Fish Fillet Sandwich. When he got to Jack in the Box, he had the whole place to himself. He parked his bike close to a large window, he didn't want to have to lock his bike but close enough so that he could guard it. As he sat by the window looking straight out at Pacific Coast Highway, he sipped his Diet Coke. He was looking at the juncture were Warner merged into PCH. It was now approaching 4:00 and he noticed that the cars were starting to increase in numbers and in another fifteen minutes, he noticed there were more and more cars until there was traffic.

He decided it was time for him to get back to his home. So, he started his trip now going in the opposite direction towards Huntington Beach's Pier. But as soon as he hit the Beach, he was surprised there were people and there were lots of them. They were coming in droves. There were dogs, there were noises, music blaring, and runners. As he drove further and further, more and more people started coming to the beach. It got too crowded for him, and it was impossible to maneuver his bike on the edge of the water because of all the people blocking his way. The sun was showing itself, shining in all her majesty. Now the fog had burned off. It was a pattern one had got used to living at the beach. There was always some kind of overcast until mid-day.

Chapter 15

A Unique Shopping Center

Within walking distance, just across the street was a unique shopping center. Every structure had a rustic appearance, a very weathered look as if everything had been bleached from the salt air. The buildings gave you the feeling that they could rust away right in front of you. The materials that the buildings were made of incorporated lots of wooden singles and fishing nets. Throughout the outside of the buildings were many metal sculptures of pelicans resting on top of large wooden poles. The basic look gave you the feeling that you were at a fishing port in a small town in New England or Nova Scotia or even Japan.

There were standard size tiles that were used for pictorial murals in the same way the Romans used mosaics. There was one mural that was 12 feet high. This mural was composed of many tiles about 10X10 inches, painted and baked on the tile were images representing cliff birds. Some of the birds where nesting on cliffs and others flying off. The wall that the tiles were mounted on was circular so that if you stood in the middle of it; you had almost Cinerama view. It seemed so realistic. Because the whole thing was made of tile, it could be exposed to the elements without effecting this creative illusion. Since the wall required natural lighting, each time he was there, he would come back with a different feeling. On overcast days, it would become almost three dimensional. The mural always took his breath away.

There were many other similar ceramic representations but nothing as large as that one. There were small little areas with displays, something you might see in a museum. Stuff birds, encased in all glass cabinets with printed information. Material on the migratory habits of the bird who visited the marsh lands of Huntington Beach and other details relating to particular species. Also on display were different paraphernalia such as hooks, arrows, and native contraptions, all following the motif of a Fisherman's Village. There was wealth of information, so much so, that he would make a point to stop and study each display. It was an unbelievable treat. It was an outside museum.

The supermarket was quite unique not inexpensive, with a Traders Joe's type of feeling with all assortments of foods. It had a bakery where bread, pastries, cakes were made daily, and a pharmacy. The shopping center also had multitude of small little craft stores sort of a miniature Laguna Beach. There was also a large auditorium type building that could be used for meetings, but it was rented out on Sunday for a Religious Science service and a small Italian Restaurant that was owned by three sisters. Of course, being Italian the whole large family where all part of the team. One of the sisters, Serafina, became one of his close friends. Right next to the restaurant was a Gold's Gym. He visited the gym ever day for his daily workout. His son, who was only fourteen, was befriended by the Italian family and given a job as a bus boy and later a waiter.

Chapter 16

Beachwalk

Standard Oil had spent a great deal of money developing this area. It was a model community that Standard Oil invested into after tapping, one by one, the multiple derricks that had covered the whole area. Beachwalk was to be built as a shared community with new style townhouses. They were not popular at that time. Gated communities were unheard of in Huntington Beach.

This fishing port motif was continued. At the center of Beachwalk, you had the clubhouse, a large predominant towering clock, Olympic swimming pool, jacuzzi, and a volleyball court. Inside the clubhouse was a fully functioning kitchen for parties, a billiard table, and a library. Most of the trees that grew behind the houses were eucalyptus, which grew rapidly and offered shade. At night, when the wind blew, they offered a soft modular sound like the ocean and an exotic smell and taste of eucalyptus. There was abundance of parking and the development of many greenbelts, something of a rarity for beach property. Across the street was a country club with an adequate golf course. Further on where acres of land for hiking with different kinds of gaming places for horseshoes and a course using a Frisbees. Not far away was the Huntington Beach Library. Within a few feet from his home were fifty tennis courts, two basketballs courts, and a softball baseball park.

Most Huntington Beach Homeowners disliked the townhouse concept, of someone restricting them on what they could do and what they couldn't. The pricing of real-estate backed this up because Beachwalk property lacked financial growth when compared to single family dwelling. But as beach property became scarce the concept of the planned community became more popular. But for him and his son, it was a hidden paradise, that many people weren't even aware of.

His son appreciated the area with lots of swimming pools, the large jacuzzi and the structured community. Michael could see that the area was building up. It was changing right in front of his eyes. It was getting more expensive to live there and it was getting crowded. He kept asking himself. If he were Jewish, lived in Berlin in 1935 while the Nazis were in power, would he have the foresight to see what was going to happen? If he were that Jew, would he have the balls to pick up and move out to another land to place where they didn't speak German? It was the only language that he spoke. Would he move to a different country and must adapt to a different culture? Give up everything and to start all over again. Would he be able to do that? Moving from Huntington Beach wasn't as drastic as it would be for that Jewish person. Beachwalk had become more than a place where he lived but he had become Beachwalk; it was his identity. It was why divorces were so difficult. You become the person you were married to. He knew things were changing and he knew he had to move. He should have sold the house when his son moved out over fifteen years ago. Now, after refinancing the place, so many times. He was living and working just to keep the house. In essence he was married to the bank.

Just the thought of moving was so painful, but he believed that the future was the present. He reasoned that it was our hang ups that prevented one from seeing what was happening. He could already see the changes that were happening. There were too many people. Now there was traffic. The experience he had at Jones Beach were now here.

He had been in paradise today; at least, as close as one can get to paradise. Where else could one be and have the beach to oneself for four hours without any other human.

He had to tell himself, repeatedly, like a mantra. "Don't forget what happened today, remember today, think of those hundreds of beautiful free pelicans. Think of the rolling waves, think of that vast ocean that was in front of you. It all belonged to you."

Yes, it would have to be left to his memory.   Like so many other things that happened to him in his lifetime. Everything was always changing. There were just too many people. It seemed to be his faith; no matter where he went, from New York to Huntington Beach, people just followed him. He felt as if he was the Pied Piper. Every year there were more and more people. He had no choice he had to move.

Chapter 17

Drucken Driver

They developed a little ritual always meeting for supper in Fullerton. There was a famous vegetarian sort of sixties restaurant where the food was delicious and healthy. She was always playful there. They would usually have a couple of liters of their wine.

Then they would continue their day by hitting some other spots in Fullerton. It didn't take very much for Poppy to get drunk. Her breath was filled with the smell of alcohol; for some reason, she couldn't oxidize alcohol efficiently. She did tell him that she was part Native American Indian and likely that was the reason why she wasn't very tolerant of alcohol. He paid the bill, and they were in exit mode. He noticed that she was struggling but that was sort of normal for her after just one glass of wine. As soon as they got to her SUV, she put one hand on the car handle and leaned over and vomited everything she just ate. She had that sick disoriented look on her face.

"Poppy, I need to drive you home."

"No, I want to drive my car home. I don't want to leave it here. My home is not that far from here. I'll take all the side streets. I'll be okay I'll be okay. I've done this before."

Yes, she did, and she got a DUI and she certainly didn't need a another one.

"Poppy, give me your keys. I'll drive your car and I'll leave my car here and I'll walk back."

If Shirley was at home, he would ask her to drive him back to the restaurant so he could get his car.

When he got into the driver's seat of her truck, he felt a little intimidated by how high he was sitting. He had to strain yourself to hit a step and then another before he got inside of this monster. He didn't find it comfortable nor something that he was used to. He didn't like driving big vehicles and no less this SUV truck. She noticed hesitancy and with a stern look on her face.

In a very unhappy tone in her voice. "Can you drive it?"

"I'm not a daredevil like you but I have driven a truck and motor home."

Slowly but surely, he started to get the hang of it. He also took the side streets just to be safe. He didn't find this monster as easy to drive as his Corolla, but he was managing it.

Finally, they got to the front door of her home. He noticed she was having trouble putting the key in; she was really struggling, and he was worried that he wasn't going to be able to get her inside. He didn't want to do it, but he knew this was the right thing to do. So, he rang the bell, and it wasn't that late, and the lights were still on. Shirley came to the door and quickly summed up the situation. Poppy flashed inside behind them, looking like a little girl caught in mischievousness.

"I drove her home in her truck because she didn't want to leave it there overnight. Would you mind giving me a lift back to the restaurant? it's only couple of miles away?"

He could see that she wasn't too happy, but he knew that she realized that he had done a good deed and he should be rewarded for it.

"All right but let me get my keys and a coat."

He could see that she had pajamas on and probably he caught her just before she was ready to sneak into bed. They went to her car, a Mercedes.

It was obvious she was angry at Poppy. "The next time to prevent this from happening make her pay for her own drinks. She is such a mooch."

They were now in her car, and she was driving.

"You know I really am sick of her. She is like an alcoholic. I can't stand alcoholics. She doesn't know when to stop drinking".

He was really startle by Shirley's comments, and he thought it sounded more like the remarks made by a jilted lover than a land lady.

"You know when she's out there she wants someone else to buy her drinks. There is one way to stop her. in one way you can stop her from drinking is just don't pay for her drinks because she'll never paid for her own drinks"

The comments that he had heard from Poppy about Shirley didn't seem to match this setup.

"She has tons of money, Christ Sake, she is the number one realtor in Fullerton and she's afraid of spending it on someone. Once and only once, did she take me to a very fancy restaurant in celebration of one of her award dinners; she landed a ten-million-dollar deal."

He felt that Poppy thought she should be sharing her money with her but for what reason. But then that was Poppy for you; she was always looking for angles.

"I pay her good money for my rent. I work at night, and I told her, you know, I need my rest. She hired some contractors to remodel the house. They make all sorts of noises, and I can't sleep."

As he drove that long trip from Fullerton to his home in Huntington Beach, he had a lot of time to think. What was he doing with this relationship or being in this relationship? He knew that Poppy was very titillating in her sexual innuendos. He felt as if one foot was in quicksand in the other foot was on dry land. If he went a step further, he would be sucked into the quicksand. And yet in the back of his head there was a part of him that knew that he could take or leave Poppy. He didn't feel that he would be heartbroken if the relationship came to an end; however, there was another part of him that was pulling him into the quicksand. He was always a dreamer and attracted to people that had problems, as if he could fix it all. She was very intelligent and there was no question about that.

He was always thrilled to go to a deep foreign movie with her. Her interpretation or her analysis of the movie was far deeper than anything he could understand or ever experience. She did live on the dark side, and he asked himself why that was so attractive to him. What did that say about him? For the most part, he saw himself as being rather conservative. But he also knew another part of him was somewhat bohemian in nature. He also knew from taking Myers-Brigg's exam that he was in the one percent of the population, being able to switch from thinking to feeling in a millisecond. He understood that he thought of his grandmothers being very wise and nonconventional. May be that's what pushed him off into this world of openness and bohemian like living.

He never had a girlfriend who was bisexual. When a pretty woman walked by them, he noticed her nostrils would flair as if she was picking up an unusual scent and her eyes got bigger. He was sort of intrigued by that. It was sort of fun to be able to look at women with her and compare notes from her perspective. They would make notes of what was attractive about their target. It would include her walk, her clothes, the style of her body, her skin, her hair, and her eyes. It was exciting to be able to share that with a woman. And she was more perceptive than he was in seeing through a female. Sometimes he felt like a child in the woods. She was his guide leading him through a forest. She knew so much and had considerable experience. In fact, he knew that she kept her connections to this world of Hollywood and parties. He was fascinated by it all who wouldn't be. She seemed to know movie stars and she related relationships that she had with some of them. He believed her because she was so matter of fact about it. He knew she had the capability to change her personality to meet the circumstances. She was a chameleon.

CHAPTER 18

Shirley Goes On Vacation And They Have The Whole Place To Themselves

Shirley went on vacation and Poppy had the whole place to yourself. It was the first time Michael was able to spend overnight and then have breakfast with Poppy. It took almost two years of dating Poppy before she finally trusted Michael enough to let him know where she lived. She was always secretive. They made love that night as usual, but this time he and she didn't have to be careful in expressing their passion while they made love. She did act sort of reserved in her own place and he could understand that. When she was at his place and she had an orgasm, the whole neighborhood could hear her screaming, "FUCK! FUCK! FUCK!".

As usual, she was up before him. He was a sleeper. In college, they would call him, Barney the Bear because he could sleep soundly. He would sleep through the whole weekend, getting up only to go to the toilet or to eat a chocolate candy bar. That was easy to understand after a snowfall in the wintery upper state New York. Blankets of snow would muffle all sounds leaving an environment that was peaceful and quiet.

She started to call him. "Get up sleepy head! Get up and join me in the kitchen. I have a surprise for you."

He sat down at the table. The table was properly set up with a tablecloth, plates, knives, forks, and napkins. Everything was perfect the coffee, the toast, the eggs, the orange juice, and different fruits. She seemed right at home acting as a perfect housewife. He was shocked and surprised to see her acting so domesticated. It was another side of her that he seldom saw. He knew how organized she was with her car where everything was clean and spic and span, all the time. But seeing her so domesticated and so happy was surprising. They sat there eating their meal, relaxed acting like two people who were an old married couple.

Later, they went out to see a movie, one of those foreign ones that they liked so much followed up at their regular pizza parlor that they liked so much. They finished off a whole pitcher of beer. They talked and talked about the movie until they were on their second pitcher of beer. He had to get up early in the morning. He drove her home. They had their brief love making and it was time to head back to Huntington Beach.

Chapter 19

Free Sex

He wondered why he wasn't jealous or trying to find out what she did with all those different men and women. In so many ways he found her actions titillating. Part of him felt excited that other people adored her and wanted her in the same way he wanted her. When they first met, she used the phrase, "Let's just hang out together." He wanted to understand that phrase. He assumed it signified a relationship that would be fluid. He wanted to experiment. He imagined that to experience those kinds of feelings; it would be devoid of the concept of property. It would be something akin to Communism.

Easier said than done. He was an only child and as he grew up, it was difficult for him to share anything with anyone. He never had to share anything. He had no brothers or sisters and whatever was his was his. Communism would be foreign to him. Yet, with Poppy, this was a strange relationship, in the sense that he wasn't infatuated with her. The truth of the matter was that he didn't want the responsibility of taking care of all her needs. His society was screwed up. If you wanted to share a woman, you had the responsibility that went with having a woman. You could rent a car; you could rent a home for the weekend. You could even go to a public library and get books, CDs and DVDs.

He knew that he couldn't afford this woman or any other for that matter. He understood that primitive man had little need for possessions. They were hunters and gathers and were always on the move. It was only after they learned how to grow food and stay in one place that possessions became part of their society.

So, in his stupidity, he was trying to cut corners. And when you did that there is always a price to pay. It was like a bill that accrued interest until you paid it off, like credit cards. You could pay forty dollars, but thirty dollars would go towards the interest and only ten dollars would go towards the principle. With Poppy, each day he would be paying the interest, but the day would come when he would have to pay off the principle. He was willing to pay the interest because that was what he could afford.

He understood that in the development of man that the Have Nots, wanted what the others had. Some societies developed rules to protect certain groups of people. He could understand that man looked for a leader, it was part of our genetic makeup. With the advent of religion and with the forming of a government, which worked together, they developed a ruling class. Someone on top ended up having a lot of possessions and power. Eventually, a society developed ways to protect those possession. Eventually followed the development of civilization as we know it. Homo Sapiens were like ants; all we must do is look at Nazi Germany. Making war on people seemed to be about certain groups protecting what they had from other groups of people, who wanted to get what they had. The losers either got killed or became slaves.

He had read that in the Lewis Clark Expedition that those explorers were astounded by those Native American's stealing ability. One of the explorers laid down his pipe and before he knew it; his pipe was gone, stolen. Those explorers would sleep with their arms wrapped around their guns and in the morning the guns were gone. It was human nature to want something that belonged to someone else. If the other person had a cigarette, he wanted one. If the other person was smoking a pipe, then the other person wanted to smoke a pipe. He understood how well primates were in their ability to copycat. Monkeys see; monkey do.

He had read how the Eskimos were willing to share their wives. They would say, "If I give my knife to someone, it will come back dull. If I give him my sleigh, it comes back damaged, but if I give him my wife, she will come back better than before."

Michael believed that Homo sapiens would need to learn how to share if they wanted to survive. In New York City, all those office buildings were empty on the weekend. If those buildings were used 24/7 rather than being shut down as they were; it would be much more efficient. When they built the Salk Institute in La Jolla, the cost of the building was thirty-three million dollars. It sat empty for many months until they could raise another thirty-three million dollars for equipment. That equipment wasn't used 24/7. It would have been wonderful if they would let the University of California San Diego, the use of the facilities, of course with a rental fee.

So, in his mind, he was trying to do this great experiment with Poppy and find out just how he would react. In the beginning, it worked because he wasn't really that infatuated with her. It seemed to work because when he went to work or had to do something; he wasn't thinking about her, nor was he concerned about her. He knew that she could take care of herself. He really wanted to make this work because he thought this was something he needed to explore. Something other humans also needed to explore. He felt the more versatile the individuals were the more they could learn. And in the end, they could contribute more their fellow mankind.

He could never understand divorce. When it was all over, why did two people fight so hard against each other. Acting as if there was still something there when there was nothing. Why couldn't they just let go? With Poppy he had no choice. He couldn't afford her full-time emotionally or financially. And yet when one got married, one was expected to satisfy his wife emotionally and financially.

There were many things to like about Poppy. She was youthful in mind and body. She was intelligent, complicated, and interesting to be with. He seemed to be drawn to those problematical women. He also knew the price for that.   What did he really have to offer them? He knew that in Poppy's case she came to him as a refuge from, The Real World.   She could take a break. She felt that she could trust him and tell him everything.   He was sort of her built-in psychologist. She knew that he was not judgmental and for her there was sex without any necessary attachments, and he accepted the relationship.

Chapter 20

The Cost Of Prostitution

He could understand why Poppy had her triple standards. He had to constantly remind himself that prostitution in the United States was frowned on and was considered a crime by many people. He assumed there were many things that Poppy had to do that were against what she believed in.

He found her sexually titillating. It was sort of the movie vs the book version. When one reads a book, one can use your imagination in creating all kinds of fanciful stuff. It was like a movie which may never be as great as what one had imagined. She gave him a lot of material to think about and to fantasy about. He led a limited exposure to life compared to Poppy. Let's face it, he was rather conservative. He had never had a relationship with a bisexual woman or someone who was not only a prostitute but mingled with the upper end of society.

But it was nice to be able to share one's sexual fantasy with someone else without any censorship. He didn't quite understand this part of himself. But he was into experimentation, and it seemed Poppy was very delicate in the way she handled their sexuality. When she was with him, she was rather conservative. From what she told him about her life, he wondered if she might not be a multiple personality. But he knew that wasn't the case because over time he would see consistency in her personality. He just accepted the fact that she was very complicated and again that was attractive to him. He was never attracted to simple easy-going women. He never saw anyone as being sane. By this time, he had convinced himself that his societies created pathways toward abnormal behavior. The proof of this was the high consumption of illegal drugs and alcohol.

Michael just assumed most of Poppy's hypochondria and her different symptoms and illnesses were due to a strong a guilt complex. Taking money from men or women was what she considered to be her Robin Hood Effect (Taking money from the rich and giving it to the poor). I'm sure she considered herself the poor person. He assumed that all her excessive shopping and buying all those clothes and things making herself looking attractive and he felt she needed that. She had rationalized that it was a necessary business expense.

Probably one of the things he found so appealing about her; she was doing so many things, that morally he could never do. In a sense her performance skirted the borders of what we might call being dishonest or crooked. They were things he was taught as a Catholic to be decadent. People did immoral things all the time. The United States exploited people all over the world and we as Americans Citizens accept that. In the same way the German people accepted slaughtering of millions of Jews while they willingly confiscated their possession for their own use. The Germans certainly considered themselves to be good Christians in the same way Americans consider themselves to be law abiding. Today, Americas develop and sell destructive weapons, killing innocent people all over the world.

Book two

Poppy's Sexuality

Chapter 1

The Opera
La Traviata (The Fallen Woman)

At the ending of the Opera, *La Traviata* (*The Fallen Woman*) by Verdi, people were getting up and leaving. As he looked over at Poppy, she had tears in her eyes. Everyone was in hurry to get out, so he sat there with her, trying to give her some protection, so she could have her private moment. He had never seen her cry before. It was not intentional that he picked this opera, a story of prostitute who finally finds her true love. You all know the ending, Violetta dies. It was the first opera of the season and he liked Verdi and *La Traviata* was Verdi's best operas. There was no hidden message on his part. It was pure chance that he had picked that opera with that story line.

He really felt sorry for Poppy. He could only imagine the hell that she went through with her triple standards. He did not look at prostitution as being a horrible thing. He understood how that life might affect a person like Poppy. She had enjoyed what the money could bring; however, another part of her felt that she was being dishonest with herself. He understood her compulsiveness, her triple standards. She wanted to be this other part of herself, but it never quite works out that way. In some ways, he envied her. He would never to be able to lead her kind of life. He couldn't even imagine that anyone would give him two thousand dollars just to have sex.

That was their first opera together but there would be many more. He liked the ambience of being at an opera. Michael felt it was like going to a football game. The audience got just as excited, shouting, and screaming.   But at an Opera, everyone was well dressed and there was a tone of aristocracy. It was the sophisticated humanity, not the low lives that one saw at sporting events. He felt sports event were too primitive for his taste.

Poppy loved going to the opera with him. It gave her the opportunity to get all dressed up, in a true courtesan style. She always managed to find a new outfit that was appropriate for the occasion.   Of course, she would always remind him of her ordeal. "You don't know what a pain it was. I had to have my hair and my nails done. I even had to go to my chiropractor. Not to mention finding the right clothes."

Her chiropractor, it was the one that Joe paid for. She always found creative ways where she could get money from her subjects. She was always buying things and one needs money to do that.

She slowly got up. Everyone was gone. She wiped her tears away and they slowly walked out.

Chapter 2

The taste of Andrea on Poppy's lips

It was several weeks later. They were at the party, at Craig's place. The apartment, that they were now in, was owned by one of Poppy's old boyfriends.

She claimed, with her typical confidence. "Oh, it was one of those very short relationships."

She squeezed her face, as if remembering or censoring what she would let him know.

"He was nice, but in the end, just not my type."

She pointed or waved at a lady, her girlfriend. Andrea was also there.

Poppy explained, "I introduced Andrea to Craig after we broke up and they lasted for quite a while, and I thought they were perfect together. I even felt that they might get married. I don't know what happened. They were together and seemed happy together. I think she just got bored with him or vice a versa. Neither one told me what went wrong but they split up as friends. It was too bad; they were so good together."

She gave him her mischievous smile. "Since I like playing cupid, I hoped it would last."

Andrea seemed to be somewhere in her late twenties. (He knew Poppy was attracted to younger women.)

Andrea was an RN and worked at the same hospital that Poppy worked at, St Jude's Hospital in Fullerton. Poppy and Andrea became close friends and did many girly things together. They both had one thing in common, severe back problems.

Michael knew that was quite common in their profession. It took a lot of strength moving either live or dead bodies from one stretcher to another. And sometimes, even moving patients around in their bed could put your back out. Changing a person's sheet while keeping the patient in their bed without moving them too much was a major strain on their backs. Not to mention that it took a certain amount of skill keeping the patient in their bed with all sorts of connections to monitors, equipment and I.V. 's. In Intensive Care, not moving the patient was sometimes the only option they had.

She also was a native Canadian American Indian; whatever that was. Being Native American allowed her dual citizenship both in Canada and the United States. She was adopted, when she was a baby, by a White Canadian Couple of better than average means. From what he heard, her adopted parents loved her. She was brought up in Western Canada and therefore that made her like a West Coast Californian. And although her background seemed somewhat exotic, she appeared quite like all the other people there. She did not look like an Eskimo or anything like that, just an ordinary California Gal.

He ended up staring at Craig, their host. The only thing that stood out about Craig, besides his rather pleasant outgoing personality. Not to mention their bodily similarity and he appeared to be a lot younger version of himself.

He noticed it right away, because it took up a large part of the room, it was his vast CD collection (in the hundreds). Poppy was quick to point out the rest of this oddity. Each CD was organized in the same way that one would see in a store or library, by the type of music that was recorded. Each case had one of those stickers from a label machine including numbers. That wasn't the end of it. He found that everything was cross referenced in a computer program listing the artist and the songs contained in the CD, cross referenced with those numbers.

Michael just couldn't imagine how someone could be that meticulous. But he was so impressed with Craig's system that for the rest of his life, he tried to replicate it. Well, at least, he himself would be able to manage his collection only to the point of labeling his CD into major categories, like Jazz and Classic music or Opera. Putting it together on computer was far beyond his capabilities. He hoped someday that he could afford a secretary and that's a task he would delegate to her.

He finally realized that Craig's whole apartment was organized in a similar way. Something, Michael assumed would be very magnetic to Poppy's compulsive neatness. Maybe Craig was too much like her in that way. He questioned her about it.

She just grunted and then smiled without saying a thing.

As the party's progressed and as more drinks were consumed. Everyone became friendlier and there was a lot of mixing going around. Poppy was moving and he liked that. So, he went in the opposite direction.

He finally bumped into Andrea. They had never talked before but by now he wasn't feeling any pain and why not. It felt easy to approach her and introduce himself. (Always remembering, what Poppy told him.)

How Poppy felt when the light was shining through Andrea's hair in that kind of certain magical moment. How Poppy felt this deep lust for Andrea. Also knowing that Poppy had trouble admitting to her lesbian desires. She never saw herself being a lesbian and was very defensive about being tagged as one. But that was part of Poppy and her triple standards. She was conflicted in everything and particularly in her sexuality. He knew that she did love men and specifically older men and particularly men who would take care of her financial needs. Needless say that these men were men that she could easily manipulate.

Being that she also liked young women was one of the winning things in their relationship. He could look at beautiful woman all day long when he was her and they would rate them. Of course, sometimes she had an advantage being a woman and she could see right through a lot of them_____ except the gals she became infatuated with. When she was infatuated, those roles reversed, and she took on the male pattern of aggressiveness and neediness.

As he looked straight into Andrea's eyes, he started with his trivial chit chat and then. "You know she was afraid to tell you but from what she told me; she is really attracted to you. She told me how you guys went camping together and she thought you were so beautiful."

Andrea's eyes lit up as he told her. "Poppy described how the light bouncing off the waterfall and flowing through your hair, in just a certain way, made you look like a goddess. She told me that she wanted to make love with you; but she wasn't sure exactly how you would take it."

She didn't seem surprised, but he could see that she was processing what he told her. He didn't think she was bisexual but assumed she knew that Poppy was. It wasn't unusual for him to blurt out secrets when he felt they were of positive nature. Besides, it was meant as a compliment. He liked telling people things, that he felt were positive.

As he looked at her, Andrea did have an attractive face, shapely, and she seemed friendly. She wasn't really his type or maybe he felt that way because she was Poppy's friend. And there was some history between Craig, now both Poppy's and Andrea's ex-boyfriend. Maybe he also felt tinge of jealousy. Unconsciously, he ruled her out and in fact he didn't even see her as a woman.

When something was forbidden, he did reaction formation thing which was really part of his passive aggressive nature. He did it with food too. A pattern he learned to do when people offered him pastries and he just moved the plate on to someone else, never seeing it.

Saying, "I don't do pastries."

It worked and he hadn't eaten ice cream in over twenty years, one of his very favorite foods. Yes, he had to constantly watch what he ate. He had one of those Slavic bodies where everything turned into fat. His daughter had the same problem and ended up being a terrible psychological problem for her. Always trying to keep her body lean.

While they were talking, he noticed a couple dragging on a joint. They were only a few feet away and when they notice that he was looking at them. They moved closer to him and offered a hit.

He was in the habit of inhaling the smoke and then passing it on to Poppy by exhaling into her while he kissed her. Since Poppy was now nearby, he made a sign. She knew what that meant, and she was next to him, and he expelled the beautiful plume into her open mouth and deep into her lungs. He then passed the Joint off to her and she in turn passed it off to Andrea.

He bought what was left of the Joint back to the compliant couple. They seem to be surrounded by a friendly bunch somewhat in the corner of the party and well set in that corner of the room. He continued his path trying to socialize with the other people always being friendly and doing his salesman personality thing. Continually talking about his writing and what he did for his living. It was his standard trivial chit-chat.

For some reason he looked back, and he couldn't see Poppy or Andrea anywhere. Suddenly, they were nowhere to be seen. If it wasn't for his buzz, he might have stayed where he was. As he looked around, he saw that the bedroom door was closed. So, he decided to open the door. As he looked inside, he really couldn't see much; but his Instinct quickly brought him to the side of the bed, and he immediately slid to the floor.

He heard Andrea say, in a somewhat questioning worried voice. "Michael is here."

Poppy responded in her low dreaming spongy sing-song voice. Her voice was hypnotics and so peaceful.

"That's fine."

He had to admit that was one of her best characteristics, she did have a sexy seductive bedroom voice. (Of course, like most women, used only when they wanted something). It was one of the reasons he wanted to meet Poppy. After talking to her on the phone, their first conversation over the phone, she used this youthful sexy tone on him, and he was seduced by it.

It seemed like only a minute, and someone opened the door. It was that lady, part of the group that gave him the Joint.

She started to scream, as if in shock, so loud that everyone in the party could hear her.

"My God, there's an orgy going on in here!"

He never undressed or even planned to. Quickly, he shot up and proceeded to close the door behind him and block anyone else from coming in. But there was no one there.

Oddly enough the party seemed to go right on as if nothing ever happened. Thank God, because the music was blaring, and besides the bedroom was somewhat tucked away from the rest of the apartment; no one heard her screaming.

He knew and understood his liberal rules especially when it concerned sex. The real world had a whole set of rules, made up by hypocrites. He believed that sex should be for pleasure and not just for procreation as he was taught by the Catholic Church.

Couldn't that lady have just opened the door just a tiny crack? After seeing just two people in the bed and another on the floor, just quietly close the door. Why did she have to scream like that?

He believed there were so many different options that woman could have taken. The door was closed. Why open it? She had to suspect that something was going on. Why else would she opened the door? Maybe she thought that they were doing coke and she wanted some. But why scream? If she was offended, she could have left the party or told Craig to police the whole thing.

Orgy? Two women on a bed and he was on the floor, fully dressed as everyone would see. He wondered if that lady really knew what an orgy was. He had witnessed a real orgy and wanted no part in it. It was animalistic event with lots of groans. But people have double standards and by the book you don't want to be at a party where people are having sex in a closed off bedroom.

Now, he glared at that woman, back in her corner with her two male friends. She did look frightened probably thinking that he was going to harm her. He wanted to go up to her. He wanted to understand what she was thinking. He just assumed she was of low class or Born Again.

Obviously, she had never been to college, where things like that occurred all the time. He remembered being at Sigma Chi while he was in college and shocked seeing the whole backyard, filled with couples flat down gyrating while lying on the grass. Of course, it was in the evening and dark; therefore, you couldn't really tell who, was who. He was shocked, but he didn't yell out.

"There's an orgy on the lawn, in the back of the fraternity!"

But now, he decided since he was only a guest, he had no rights while at Craig's party to do anything. And he didn't want to make a scene and make matters worse for Poppy and Andrea.

Poppy finally showed up, nonplussed. He smiled and reached down to give her a kiss. He could taste and smell Andrea's juices. It excited him a lot and he didn't know why. She was sharing her trophy; like a cat would do for his master. He could feel and see that she liked the effect it had on him. He thought that it showed her male character. Afterall, part of the fun of having sex, at least for most males, was the conquering aspect and control. And being in control was so typical of Poppy. He saw and understood; that in the end, she always wanted to be in charge.

Chapter 3

Poppy Blames Michael For Her Sexual Time With Andrea

Sometime later. In fact, several days later. They met.

She had her face all squared off.

"You compromised me at that party. I am really pissed at you. You set me up with that drag of marijuana! And Andrea told me what you said about me."

It wasn't worth arguing with her, when she went into one of her moods, followed by her bombastic lectures using her triple standards. He only wished he could have been that devious or clever. She should have thanked him. He witnessed that satisfied look she had on her face when she proudly kissed him and purposely exhibited Andrea's pussy smell all over her face. And then that look, he would learn, when she had conquered someone.

Some weeks later, she told him in her matter fact tone of voice with her typical bit of sarcasm in her voice.

"Andrea wants me to take her to an orgy." Then with a kind of anger. "She said, she had her, **'Fucking Red High Heels'**, ready to go."

He really wasn't that surprised by this message. That she was going to explore a sexual relationship with Andrea. In fact, he was somewhat pleased, because it once more reinforced what he had learned about her that she was full of shit. She would say one thing, then do the opposite thing. But he realized that was part of her sickness. The conflict of what societies tells us is right or wrong, doesn't always hold true for her. He saw what this conflict had done to her mentally. Using your body for profit had it's downside. He felt that was why she was always in so much physical pain. He felt that was one of the problems with prostitution in the states, it was treated as a criminal act.

Of course, it was no secret he felt our cultural attitude about our sexuality was fucked up. He was much too much a Connecticut Conservative to have led the life that Poppy led. But he enjoyed seeing that she could experiment and play outside societies stupid rules. Of course, he was interested in hearing about her experience and couldn't wait to hear all the dirty details. It would be very titillating for him to just to think about what would happen. Knowing Poppy, she wouldn't spare him the details. Doing something that is forbidden and getting away with it was always entertaining. He knew a bit of what she would be doing. He had only one similar experience, that is, going to a sex party, and he knew how it would work out.

Chapter 4

Orgy Time / Oh My?

One party was more than enough for him. It was quite a while ago and he would never forget it.

But he had to be interviewed to see if he would be even invited. The first step, he had to be interviewed by the leader of the group. He knew Poppy didn't have to go through an interview because she knew people and all she needed to do was make a phone call.

When he got there, he was so surprised, because it was a regular looking house in a very residential area. All the lawns were immaculate and the whole area was free from any trash. He estimated that those homes were worth over a million dollars. The point being it was not in some sleazy area, just an ordinary neighborhood.

Of course, he had an appointment, it felt like he was visiting a doctor. In fact, it was his psychologist who recommended this venture. When he rang the bell, the door was almost immediately opened and a tall thin man in his fifties greeted him with a pleasant unarming smile. He immediately introduced himself as Gary.

They ended up in an office___ desk and all. There was the usual ice breaking introduction. He learned that he was in fact a psychologist.

"I'm glad we had a chance to meet. I just want to give you a run down on our rules and regulations. Have you ever attended a sex party before?"

Guiltily, "No, this my first time."

"Good, well, it's like any other party. We have drinks, music and lots of TV, movies for stimulation"

(He assumed he was talking about X-rated stuff). "The most important thing, you must leave any of that macho stuff on the outside. We are not interested in anyone who's super macho. But then, you don't strike me as being that kind of person."

He wasn't quite sure what he meant about being macho, but he assumed he was referring to someone who was very vanilla.

In a somewhat defensive mode. "No, I have a pretty long line of psychology behind me."

Michael threw in a few caveats about his psychology background including his master's in clinical psychology and his earlier experience as a technician in a Neurophysiology Research Laboratory at the Institute of the Living

With a shrug of his shoulders and a big smile. Besides, I'm a salesman and we are fairly adaptable."

Now Gary had even bigger smile and continued. "Well let me take you around the place so you can get a sort of general idea of the setup we have here."

They walked by a rather large room and Gary said. "This is our rumpus room or playroom."

He smiled again. "For newcomers like yourself. I would recommend that you stay outside of the room and just watch. Of course, on your first visit, you will have a guide and she will set you up and introduce you to the other guest. We want you to feel relaxed and we want to make you feel comfortable."

A little change in pace.

"I would recommend that you wear something that is easy to get in and out of. A lot of people like to wear shorts."

He knew exactly what he would wear. It was made of terry cloth like material, it was a towel (with a button on the top).

"One other thing, after your first visit, you need to come with a person. Only this once, we will get you an escort, but the next time, you will have to bring your own partner. It's that age old testosterone problem; there are always more men who want to do this thing than women."

Well, Michael got through the orientation. Now all he had to do is wait for the weekend. But the weekend was coming up fast and he was getting nervous. Not just nervous but really nervous. Soon enough, he was there knocking at the door, ready for his little adventure. He brought a couple bottles of wine and felt he might be the one who would drink it all. The door started to open, and he was greeted by an attractive lady in her early forties. She was trim and with a good-looking figure. They went through the typical introductions.

Joan smiled. Since you are so early, we have time to take you on a little tour.

They walked upstairs where there was a bunch of rooms (private little cubicles) that looked like stables with beds.

He looked at his tour guide, Joan and anxious to get things going. "Well, there's not that many people. Can we do it together?"

She laughed, "Sure, why not, as you said there's not too many people here and you are just learning."

He still had his regular clothes on, and she pointed to locker where he got undressed.

They both were now undressed, and she had quite exquisite looking body. He liked a little bit of fore play so he played with her breasts and did his natural licking the pussy routine which he thought he was pretty good at. All that trumpet playing paid off. Then, they had the old-fashioned kind of sex.

When they were finished, she was in a hurry to get back to her job. By this time, the rooms were filling up and all of the TV consuls had X-Rated flicks playing. There was crowd now. Lots of buzzing. A bell started to ring, and everybody came into one room altogether, skimpily dressed up.

Gary started to speak. He went into something resembling the reading of minutes that one would expect at formal meeting. After he was finished with the minutes, he started quoting the rules and regulations. Then he went into some kind a little sermon. He felt it was rather lengthy but than it was sort of a club. He was surprised with the ending; it was sort of a prayer, a good spirit send off.

Everyone said a little prayer and then the bell rang for the last time.

He said. "Let the fun begin." And like horses they were all off and running. He was sitting on a couch with another couple, they seemed to be married. Out of nowhere, a young gal, good looking, raced toward them. Right in front of them, with a big smile on her face, she started taking off all her clothes. She obviously knew the couple that he was sitting next to. Without any chitchat, she starts kissing the woman. They quickly disappeared. There was a lot of that going on and it seemed that everybody paired off rather quickly. And now the room was empty and there and no one left. He was all by himself. He felt rather loss and decided to go see the pool area. There was a couple sitting there and he decided to join them. They smiled at him but that was it. He felt sort of embarrassed sitting there without any clothes on. He tried to act relaxed but that got hard to do. So, he went back to the big room. He thought that maybe a glass of wine would relax him.

He finally saw someone standing by herself, a young black lady, in her early twenties.

"Are you having a good time?"

"Yes, I am having wonderful time. Gary suggested that I try this out for therapy. I was raped recently, and I was having a hard time getting over it. I built up a negative attitude about having sex with someone. I think this is working."

Before he could say another word, another guy came along. It seemed to be someone that she seemed to know. She took off with him.

It was getting rather boring. Then he saw a very sexy woman and she was sitting on a sofa and watching one of those X rated movies and she was all by herself.

I guess someone saw him looking. "She's with her husband here but she doesn't get involved in the sexual stuff.

She just sits there waiting for him so they can go home together."

He went by the orgy room, The Big Room, and he absolutely couldn't investigate The Big Room, the one you're not supposed to go into unless you are ready to go all the way. He was too private for that, and he was even afraid to look in. He couldn't even stand by the door. By now he was very bored, and he went home and took a very long shower.

Chapter 5

Finding Fault With Andrea

"Andrea and I made sure we had purchased enough rubbers. She was so proud of her damn fucking red high heels!"

He couldn't help noticing the way Poppy said," fucking red high heels." She seemed angry when she repeated those words. Poppy was acting as if she had found some imperfection in Andrea. He watched the expression on her face. There was disgust in her voice, and she looked straight ahead. He had learned what that meant, her looking straight ahead like that, in sort of trance. He was guessing that Poppy finally realized just how straight, Andrea was. She was a lot younger than Poppy. Michael had guessed that Poppy had learned that Andrea wanted to have a baby and a man to take care of her. Andrea was probably dumped by Craig, because he didn't want to get married and he didn't want to have a brat to put up with in his orderly world.

Poppy patted the seat next to him. "She wanted to have one guy fucking her while the other guy fucked her up her ass. She padded the end of the bed. She told me she wanted me sitting there, right next to her while she was being fucked!"

Sort of laughing to himself and then joking. "Did you enjoy yourself? You must have let someone suck your tit or something?"

" I wasn't in the mood but yes I did let the guy play with me and my tits."

From that moment on, almost like the actions of a jilted lover; she showed more negativity as if building a case against Andrea. A month later, he was surprised to hear. "Andrea and I did it with Joe. I really can't remember too much of what happened. I was so drunk; all I know is Joe really enjoyed it. He just keeps talking about wanting to do it again."

He knew her. He felt that she knew what happened but in complicated way censored it out the same way he pretended not to see dessert or ice cream when it was served to him. He also knew she liked playing one against the other and in this case trying to make him jealous. But he had learned not to go for the bait. He did notice that play was happening more often.

Chapter 6

Checking For Aids

He wasn't quite sure why they had decided to go to the Orange County Public Health Laboratory and have an Aids Test. It probably was something they were both curious about since they both had many sex partners over the years. It probably felt better to have company, to have someone with you; yet they drove there in separate cars.

They called her in first and then he was called. When he came back to the waiting room after the public health person had asked him a bunch of very personal questions and finally drew his blood. To get the results, he needed to come back in a few weeks. When he got back to the waiting room, she was no longer there. She hadn't even waited for him, and he wasn't quite sure what that meant.

He finally got her on her home phone and asked. "Why didn't you wait for me?"

Her response was somewhat sarcastic, "Well I have AIDS."

He knew now that their planned lunch together was cancelled. She was angry at him for even recommending having the tests done. The fact that she had been a prostitute and seemed to be with so many different people both male and female, he couldn't understand why she was acting the way she was. But he knew that was Poppy for you. She had her own rulebook, and he was such a novice compared to her that it was only fair that he should have been concerned about AIDS. He knew she was fastidious when it came to sexual intercourse. But he also knew that she operated on her triple standards. Her rules for him were a lot higher than the rules she applied to herself. Unfortunately, part of his attraction for her was that she was so much more mature or exposed to this other side life. She was street smart. He was never exposed to so many different angles of life. He just never lived on the edge in the way she did. His mind and imagination might have drawn him into that world, but his conservative personality would eventually stop him before he got much further into what he considered the criminal world or the perverted immoral world.

Chapter 7

Poppy's Closet

As a little boy, Michael was annoyed with his mother when she would drag him with her to her different dress stores. Of course, he would have to sit there on a bench, in complete boredom, while she tried on different dresses.

His mother would say this over, and over.

"Someday, someone will thank me for training you like this."

And she was correct. When he was married, he had acquired a good eye for buying clothes for a woman. With his Christmas bonus, he would end up buying all kinds of clothes for his wife. Those clothes would include matching shoes, handbag, shirts, blouses, and a winter jacket. When he was done, picking out all those nice things, he noticed how impressed all the saleswomen were with his ability of putting it all together. In one case, one of the sales ladies was so impressed that she asked him if he would take her home for Christmas.

Of course, his shopping was a great success, and his wife was more than pleased in having all those nice new clothes. Not only did she have a great addition to her plain assortment of clothes;

but she received multitudes of praises from her fellow nurses for her unique look.

Now so many years later, it was not uncommon that he and Poppy would be dashing into different boutiques, those many expensive stores at Newport's Fashion Island. He enjoyed it, Poppy parading and modeling the different dresses. In fact, it was one of those favorite things he liked doing with her. He understood how different clothes could bring out different parts of a person's personality. He loved seeing the transformation that overtook Poppy. Every dress made her become a different person.

He was amazed how she would shop from one dress to another and then back to the same dress. Some of the time, it could become frustrating. It occurred over her indecision whether she wanted to buy this one type of a summer green dress. She went back and forth, putting it on off over five times. It became monotonous.

Finally, she asked him. "Which one do you like. Which one looks the best on me?"

He picked the green dress.

Now, the ritual that followed was always the same. She would give the salesclerk a small deposit, with a look, that he was familiar with. It was the look of someone who was greedy. He saw it on a lot of gambler's faces, when the winnings were going their way and they were ready to place what they felt would be their next winning bet.

Then, she would speak with her authoritative business voice. "Please, put it on layaway." There was a pause, as she counted out several crispy twenty-dollar bills. "I will be back with the balance in the next couple of days."

She never used credit cards; all her transactions were in cash.

Months later, they were in her bedroom, she rolled open the sliding door of the closet and he was amazed to see so many dresses and even some of the dresses that he and she had picked out. He was surprised to see that some were still in their original plastic bags with all their price tags still intact. In the corner, was the green dress that they spent hours looking at. That dress was in its' original wrapping with its' price tag. It was untouched.

She noticed that he was staring at those dresses with their price tags that were still in place.

Her response was: "Well sometimes, I just decide that I don't want to wear a dress and I trade it in."

"Do you get the full price when you trade it in?"

"Not quite, but I have a lady that I deal with that will accept the dresses, almost at full price. And she gives me cash."

As he glanced at the floor of the closet, he noticed several pairs of shoes. It was amazing that there were several pairs that were identical. The only difference were their colors. From his perspective, if he had the money, he would never repeatedly buy the same pair of shoes. It was rather something he now knew was an idiosyncrasy of the rich.

He thought of his roommate in college, Ed. He came from a very wealthy home that was in Greenwich, Connecticut. His parents gave him a new Lincoln which he drove around campus. That was different from the other college guys who had little small sports cars. Even Brock Yates, (Cannon Ball Run) only owned a spiffy MG. There were others, who owned Triumphs and one or two other students who owned the more expensive, his favorite Austin Healey. But Ed went one step further and out did them all. He flew almost every day. Renting planes which must have cost Ed a small fortune. He had a pilot license and Michael guessed that

Ed wanted to show his skills off. Flying a plane almost every day was quite a power trip for a sophomore in college.

There were a few times, Ed would let him be his passenger. They flew low over the campus. Letting everybody know who they were. It was quite a rich experience for Michael. He remembers looking down, buzzing the college campus. They weren't much higher than a twenty-story building, sometimes they even flew a bit lower if Michael egged him on.

The campus looked magnificent from that height especially with Seneca Lake in the background. It all looked so tiny against the geometric patterns of the street, making everything look artificial. It looked like the layout of a miniature railroad. The trees looked too symmetrical, and the grass looked like someone colored the brown soil with a green paint. Nothing really looked real from that height.

On one of those college breaks, Ed decided to take him home to Greenwich, Connecticut and from there Michael could grab a train to, New Britain. As they approached his home. He was dumbfounded by the driveway; it could have been a regular street. The driveway went on for quite a bit. He noticed that in the background that there were five or six groundworkers, on the facility. When he got into his home, he was sort of shocked because all the furniture looked old and dilapidated. The only thing modern was the stereo and the TV.

Ed grabbed him and said. "Let me show you something."

He brought them into his mother's bedroom and Michael saw on the bed and a bedspread and directly in the center of the bedspread was a big tan stain.

Proudly, with his chest puffed up, Ed pointed to the stain. "That's where Marie Antoinette spilled her tea."

Michael finally got it, that dilapidated furniture was worth thousands of dollars. They were antiques. So much for the rich, they lived by totally different standards.

After the Christmas break, Ed loaded his dormitory's closet with lots of new clothes that he purchased at Sak's Fifth Avenue. He noticed that he had bought three angora black sport jackets, all identical. Ed opened a very large box and there were ten white shirts that were also identical.

That's when he learned early in life that people with money had strange buying habits. He could only assume that she was like his college roommate. Being an expensive call girl, she was used to lots of money, and she also associated with people of that rich class who had a lot of money.

Being in front of those dresses, Poppy was now really going into one of her good moods. "Do you mind if I try them on and show you how I look?"

She then proceeded to put on one outfit after another and paraded in front of the mirror. Like an actress, she changed with each new dress. She rotated and modeled the clothes. As she swirled around, he noticed how well defined her calf muscles were. She didn't wear high heels that often and so now he realized how attractive her legs were. He always found a woman's legs to be one of the most attractive parts of a woman's anatomy. Unfortunately, there were few women that had well defined legs. Unlike breast, legs were always on full display whenever a woman wore a skirt.

The next thing he noticed is that there were several black tuxedo type outfits in the closet.

"What do you do with those?" He pointed to the tuxedos.

"Oh, they're leftovers from my limousine days. I found it appropriate to wear a tuxedo. It gave me bigger and better tips."

"I like to see what you look like in that tuxedo."

She modeled them all. The tuxedos were skintight. She had a slim figure and she looked rather exotic in them giving her that unisex appearance that he learned excited her.

She could see that he was under her spell and with cockiness she explained.

"Some guy gave me two thousand dollars; just so he could talk with me. Another time, one client had given me a very expensive fur coat. We were close. I got pissed off at something he did to me that I threw the coat in the fireplace, and I burned it, right in front of him." The burning of the coat seemed to be something right out of Fyodor Dostoevsky's Novel.

He shook his head thinking to himself. Yes, rich people have peculiar taste.

Sometime later, he was driving her and witnessed her taking three dresses to a shop around the corner from her place in Fullerton. He just sat there in the car watching her. He was feeling hurt because that green dress was one among three that she was returning. She never wore it.

She quickly come out sprinting towards him, acting like a little girl, with a big smile on her face and cash in her hand.

"She gave me the full price for everything."

Chapter 8

Embarrashing Moments Or Childhood Conditioning

He was just mesmerized by Poppy's complex personality. In many ways, it helped him understand his own personality and his own motivations. He was always interested in some of his own neurotic behavior. His firm belief was that we developed those patterns in early childhood.

He started to notice that when he went into the supermarket or any library, his problems would begin. His gut would start turning on him and he would get this awful painful feeling. He wanted to go to the bathroom. RIGHT NOW!

He tried to control these movements in his gut, but they would continue, and they would get sharper and more painful. And he knew that he might have an accident. Now, he was so aware of what was happening. He didn't want to have an accident. So, he ran to the Men's Room and just in time.

The first time that happened, he held back the pain and spasm. When he got to the checkout counter, he felt something unusual. As he was walking out, to his surprise an embarrassment a little fecal ball rolled down the inside of his pants and down on the floor. He looked around quickly to make sure no one noticed and picked it up and ran out of the store as fast as he could.

He discussed this experience with his psychologist, who he frequented from time to time, just to make sure he was going in the right direction. Duane sort of laughed understanding how embarrassing the accident was. But never went any further with any explanation. Eventually, for his own protection, whenever he started feeling those grumbles and spasms; he would run to the bathroom without fighting it. He just couldn't find a reason why this happened every time he went to the to the supermarket.

He realized that in his childhood that his mother, liked to go shopping and she wanted to have him as her escort. She insisted on having him standing next to her while she did her shopping at different department stores. This was very boring for him. He developed a strategy to get away by needing to go to the bathroom. After he was done in the bathroom, he would take a straight course to the Toy Department. Of course, she caught on to this, and it worked out to be a good tactic. It was okay with her because at least she knew where he was. She would meet him at the Toy Department.

He realized like in dreams the message was camouflaged. With some study one would see the connection. So here it was, he had developed this pattern early in life. He could see similar patterns with Poppy's many disturbances. The pattern where some little childhood incident that was turned around and twisted to the point that it was almost impossible to find the connection to the original stimulus causing the neurosis.

Chapter 9

Creating Good Habits

As they were driving home.

"Do you mind if you drop me off at the Post Office? I need to check my mailbox."

By now he was used to her secretiveness. Of course, she would use a mailbox, so no one would know her address. I'm sure she was afraid that Shirley might look through her mail. Poppy was all about secrets.

She got out of the car, and he watched as she thrust herself towards the post office. Her stride was always interesting to observe. She took long strides, and her posture was erect making her look taller. She appeared to be confident in her movements, one step at a time. She didn't shuffle the way he did, and she just took large, long big steps.

She did not come out immediately; so, he wondered what was going on. He decided to go inside the post office to see what was the hold up. He saw her in the corner of the building hanging over a trash bucket, going over each letter carefully and then throwing each one away.

She looked at him and smiled. "Most of these are advertisements. I always do this; I don't want to take a whole bunch of junk home. In this way, I eliminate most of the stuff right away. I end up with what I need to keep."

He thought to himself, how clever she was and from that time forward he learned to do the same thing. She was a master at organization and putting everything into its proper place. He wanted to learn to be thorough and wished his college had courses on how to organize yourself. She did so many little things that were clever. Another habit she had with her socks when she took them off her feet; she would use a safety pin to keep them paired together before they were dumped into the washing machine.

"See I don't have to match them afterwards and I never lose them that way."

He started to do the same thing and she was right, from that time forward he never lost any socks.

Chapter 10

His Shit

But he started to understand what the future with Poppy would look like.

He kept telling himself. "Wake up!!! She is fickle. And no one person would ever fill her needs."

He should feel happy having that kind of insight. But he always felt that love was like a drug, and it took a while for it to wear off. He was still under her influence but thankfully, he was coming up and out. And as in so many turns in life, the right move is painful. Every relationship makes one grow. And right now, the first thing on his list of things to do was to sell his home and get out of Dodge City.

All those twists and turns of life. Painful lessons mixed in with hindsight. It always works out to be a good path for his soul. He had been accepted to New York Medical (Flower Fifth) and Chicago Medical School. Yes, he was accepted but because of his D in physics although he deserved at least a C, he would be on probation if he accepted.

New York Medical School was a good school, and they were known, renowned for turning out average academic students into very good physicians. Unlike Yale, which turned out great research physicians with little bedside manners. He would constantly hear it from the brightest students at Hobart with comments like: "God you're so bright and yet you're so dumb."

He had trouble with numbers particularly when using a slide rule. It wasn't very easy to determine where the decimal point went and that was very critical particular in physics. Of course, he deserved at least a C in that class. He had a great lab score and great hour exam score. The head of the Physics Department comment. "If he can't get his decimal points right, he doesn't deserve to be a doctor."

It was no secret to him that he was challenged by a learning disability (probably some kind of dyslexia. That bastard gave him zeros on his quizzes because most of the time he had his decimal point in the wrong place even though he had the correct answer. That head of the department, Dr. Hause, an unknown professor, who thought he was a big shot because he worked with Michelson. He was the first to determine the speed of light. He didn't like the professor and the professor didn't like him but that was college for you.

It was a long haul from medical school to the career he wanted which was in psychiatry. He could have been a great psychiatrist. But if that happened and knowing his personality, Michael would have been so impressed with himself that he probably won't have been a great person. Most likely he would have ended up in New York City. He would have been close to his family and that would not have been good. Later in his life there were many other similar opportunities. Each one of those miss-moves caused him great pain but great personal growth

Chapter 11

Meeting Poppy's Family

He wasn't sure why he was pushing to meet her family. He was caught up into making a commitment to her. He wanted her to know that he wanted her. As far as her family were concerned, she was really in another relationship. They had a five-year relationship with Joe and his son. Michael could feel that her mother felt that Joe would take good care of her. When Michael analyzed the whole thing, Joe as a police officer probably made more money than he did and could take better care of Poppy.

He was learning that Poppy was extremely fickle, but that thought was in another part of his brain. He wasn't listening to it. He was so happy to be here with Poppy. They had found this sort of old deserted motel that hung over a cliff on the ocean in the City of Ventura. Their room was right on the ocean and there was nothing better in the whole wide world than the smell of salt water. Nothing could duplicate the sound of the magical lapping and roar of the waves when one was in bed ready to fall into deep quiet peaceful sleep.

He was being persistent on meeting her mother. WHY?

"You know my mother loves this place. They spent a lot of days at this very hotel."

He was thinking that if he were to meet her mother, this might be the perfect place and time to do it.

"What if we asked your family to come out here for lunch? Do you think they would since this is one of their favorite spots? I think that might workout. What do you think?"

"I could call them and see if they would be interested. I know they love this place. Do you really want to do it? do you really want to meet my family?"

"Why not. The timing is perfect."

She made the phone call. They didn't hesitate. But he seemed to notice a transformation in Poppy. They had a lot of time before her family would show up. They had some to be alone and they ended up at the bottom of the cliff, getting their feet wet, going in and out of the water. They followed the movement of the waves. While they were enjoying the splashing of water on their legs; they were discussing the pros and cons of having her family joining them. They carried on with their debate and as she played in the ocean. She seemed to be transformed to a younger thirteen-year-old teenager. It seemed as if she was regressing, especially when she was talking about her mother. She looked rather pale in her face as if this meeting was a big decision. He was really puzzled over her relationship with her mother. He could understand and accept that any person would have a special place for their mother. But he sensed that there was something here that resembled codependence.

Shortly, they got a call on her cell that they had arrived and that they would be in the restaurant. Sure enough, there they were sitting at very long table with the mother at the very top of the table. When he saw her mother, her stepfather, and her sister, he was shocked. They looked like something that was run over by a steamroller. Poppy never told him that her father-in-law was black. Her mother seemed unattractive, small, and extremely plump. He didn't like the clothes she was wearing. Although her sister seemed excited and very friendly. She jumped out of her chair to greet them. She wasn't very attractive.

The stories he heard from Poppy, was that her mother was once hospitalized in a sanitarium for mental illness.

"My father had to come home to take care of her. He was in the military, and he had to take an emergency leave and have her committed. He told me the whole story after I found the documents hidden in one the dressing room drawers. He told me she was in an insane asylum. Of course, I didn't believe it until I read all of the document. Those documents validated the fact that she was a patient at an insane asylum.

I know my mother married my father too early. She was only sixteen years old. She wanted to get away from her father so badly that she ran after any man that would take her. She wanted to be a singer and she was a very good singer and for the next two years she sang at different bars. I'm not sure my father liked that."

As he looked at her family, he was beginning to get cold feet and was beginning to wonder what he was really doing. Later, when he went to the men's room and the father-in-law, Ron joined him. Michael liked Ron because he was friendly and seemed unpretentious. In their conversation there was an innuendo that this was one crazy family. Michael felt that the message was loud and clear and that he should save himself by running in the opposite direction.

Chapter 12

The Magical Night

Her family was gone and now they had the night together. Deep in their tranquility sipping on their wine. They sat on the lawn, watching a beautiful sunset.

It was dark when they got to their bedroom. they had this marvelous hideaway. There is nothing more relaxing or romantic than hearing the rolling in and the bubbling and the roar of the ocean, the power of Mother Nature That finally smacking sound when the wave hits land. There could be nothing more magnificent than that. They both loved water, and this was the perfect place for them. The wonderful rolling noise of the ocean waves and even the smell of the salt in the air it was hypnotic.

They were happy and even more so after they finished a joint. It was late now, but they were ready to have sex. As usual he had his plentiful amount of marijuana. He had become quite skilled at growing marijuana in his backyard, and it seemed that he had always a crop ready for all of the seasons. He couldn't afford the drugs that Poppy was into. He couldn't even afford coke, nor did he want to spend his money for that drug. He found coke to be a far too expensive. He felt the high was too short-lived. He had done a lot of amphetamines when he was younger. He had been a pharmaceutical salesman and used large amounts of diet pills for dieting. Those pills had so many side effects after while it wasn't worth, the bad breath, tachycardia, sleepless nights and sometimes the loss of control of one's temper. He knew Poppy loved coke of course he knew she liked all the opiates.

He decided to play a game. He got a mirror, a razor blade and rolled up a dollar bill. He made a tapping noise on the glass as if there were lines of coke. He took the dollar bill and put it into his nose, and he sniffed the imaginary line. He repeated the whole process, and she did the same thing. With the help of the marijuana and the liquor and their imagination they were off and running.

He was the first one to undress and jump into the bed. She joined him quickly. He liked touching her and feeling her soft skin.

"I love looking at your eyebrows. You have a little bumpy ridge, right here, that makes you look exotic."

With his finger, he touched that part of her face softly.

"Must be part of the Indian in you."

She smiled. "Yes, it's the Indian part of me. I'm glad you like it."

He started to kiss her ever so gently.

"I love your lips and every part of you is in perfect proportion. I love smelling your hair."

As he kissed her, he started sticking his tongue into her open mouth. He was a bit surprised when she vigorously started to tongue him back and biting his lips. She then went into a kind of frenzy and ripping his back with her fingernails. That was one of the things he liked about her. It was her energy.

She had reminded him from time from time. "After someone has sex with me, they can never go back. They know that they have had the best fuck of their life."

He knew that one of her favorite positions was to be on top of a man. He liked that too. He knew that he didn't have one of the longest penises. Once he was inside of woman and in that position, he would never slip out. One of his ex-girlfriends called it, the lazy man's fuck, because the woman did all the work.

Poppy was like a machine moving in all kinds of positions and he felt like his cock was captured into some kind of vice. He was never one to come quickly and he didn't tonight. She seemed to be in rare form, and she just kept going. He loved seeing that energy in her and wildness. He finally turned her over as she bit him viciously while drawing blood and digging in deep, scratching him with her long, elegant fingernails. He was caught up in her frenzy of unconsciously bit her as much as she had bit him.

They both seemed to extend their excitement over and over.

With her hot breath, she whispered in his ear.

"You know I can make you have multiple orgasms."

They both enjoyed oral sex and now he used it on her so he could catch his breath and have some time to restore himself. They slashed out at each other like wild animals. Biting each other. Screaming and yelling, he never experienced frenzy like this before. During all their frantic loving, in the background one could hear the power of breaking waves. They made love all night long listening to the roaring ocean as they made their grunts and groans and expiration of wonderful feelings brought on by one sexual orgasm after another. They lost all sense of time until they saw light coming through the windows. By then, they were both spent and fell asleep in each other arms.

He heard running water and reached over for her realizing that she was taking a shower, but he immediately fell back to sleep. When he awoke, he felt hungry and could smell the fresh brewed coffee. The room had one of those coffee makers. He saw Poppy all dressed and sitting at a desk writing, in deep concentration. He assumed she was writing one of her poems.

"I guess it's time to get up. I feel like I could eat a horse."

She was in total concentration and said. "Ah-huh."

He jumped into the shower. Not until after shaving, while looking into a mirror, did he see all the scratches and the black, blue marks all over his body.

He jumped out of the bathroom. "Boy, look what you did to me last night."

She didn't look up and it was then he noticed that both sides of her neck were covered with hickeys.

"Looks like I did a job on you too."

The hickeys were going to be difficult to explain to Joe or Shirley. They were quite embarrassing marks on both of their bodies. He also knew when all the good feelings worn off; she would be very angry at him because she didn't want Shirley of all people to see her this way.

"I'm going to have to wear a lot of cover makeup for some time. Get dressed; I'm hungry, too!"

While driving home, she kept saying." God, I think I want to marry you. I had such a wonderful time. It was really beautiful."

As he drove, time stood still. Finally, they were now at her place. They both seemed tranquil and hesitated to say goodbye. He sort of got to know Poppy and he realized that he had to measure what she said like a grain of sand. He knew that as soon as he closed his car door and drove away; she would change. She would get involved with something else. She was a chameleon and changed from one situation to another

As he predicted the real world would slowly intercede. Days passed now with her busy exhausting twelve-hour shifts. He had his days, working around the clock with Charlie at a Bakersfield's Refinery where they almost blew themselves up because of a malfunctioning degassing machine. That evening became just another one of their magical moments together that would eventually become a faint memory.

Poppy And Going To Big Bear

It was the day before their trip was going to take place, she called him.

"We need to cancel the trip because I have a severe case of pneumonia. I had a long discussion with my mother, and she insisted that I shouldn't go to Big Bear, and she said that my pneumonia would get worse if I go to such a cold place."

"Wait a minute, we have been planning this trip for months and it was your idea not mine. There are no refunds at this late date. You don't have to go outside, and I can keep you bundled up."

"My mother doesn't care. My mother insists that I shouldn't go and I should listen to her. You know she doesn't trust you."

"Let me talk to her and I can explain. It's not like we are going skiing."

"I don't want you talking to my mother! My Mother insist that she knows what is right for me and I shouldn't expose myself to the cold."

He knew that her mother didn't like him or trust him. It really bothered him because he didn't think that much of her mother either. He saw her mother as being a low-class person. She was short, fat and very homely. She was very dictatorial and bossy. With a mother like that, he knew why Poppy was so fucked up. Besides, where was she all those years when her daughter was a hooker.

He kept insisting that he would take care of her and bundle her up. That they would stay indoors all the time and he would keep her warm with a nice fire that would be going all the time. He felt it would be even good for her to be there because he would be able to nurse her and take care of her. He worked with patients before and he knew how to be a good nurse. He had been a Navy Corpsman, and he was used to treating sick people. Everything would be fine, and he would not expose her to the cold air.

He finally talked her into making the trip by insisting that if she didn't want to go, or couldn't go, that she should pay him back half of the thousand dollars that he had spent on the reservation. They finally decided to take her SUV since it was a four-wheel drive, and it could negotiate up there if there was any snow. And if they were lucky, it might snow. He had never been to Big Bear in the wintertime with the snow on the ground and this would be a treat for him. It would remind him of the good times in the winter at his home in Connecticut.

It was a new day and the day of the trip and now he was waiting for her to come over to his place to pick him up. She finally got there. He knew that he was being impatient. He was excited; he never spent an overnight at Big Bear. She had made such a big deal about how wonderful Big Bear could be in the middle of the winter and he was hoping that it would turn out to be as thrilling as she made it out to be.

She was on time as usual, and he shouldn't have worried. He made her back up her SUV so that he could open the garage doors and then he got the wood out of the garage and into the back of her vehicle. He had accumulated a lot of wood for just this, and other paraphernalia that they would use while they were in the cabin. He packed it in. When he was done, he had managed to load up the whole back end of the SUV with all the wood. He didn't want to freeze up there. They were now all set and he managed to close the trunk door just before he climbed into the front seat. She was going to do the driving.

She had that sourpuss look on her face that he had gotten used to. He didn't exactly know how to describe the expression on her face. He just called it, her sour face look. "I'm pissed off and I'm going to let you know it." She used it when she wanted to bully you into doing something that she wanted or didn't want. Or," I'm going to give you a command and I want you to do what I'm telling you." Or "I'm not happy with the situation and you better pay attention to me."

Poppy and he were planning this trip for some time, and he felt that it was a lot of money for a three-day stay at Big Bear. Since the unit was just a few feet from the frozen lake and it was at the high season, it wasn't cheap.

He tried to break the ice. "Poppy, I guarantee it. It will be a good trip. It'll be fine. We'll take care of you. You shouldn't have anything to worry about."

They finally got on the freeway, and she still didn't say a word and he didn't say a word. They were both just smoldering in anger.

It was obvious to him from the way she drove that she was very familiar with Big Bear. His impression was that she had been there many times. He guessed that she knew all the shortcuts because she had frequent Big Beer so many times. She said that she was even considering buying a cabin out there. She found short cuts that weren't even on the map. As the road got winding, it meant that they were getting close. She finally came out of her funk mood and started to talk to him. He was angry at her in the way she seemed to be telling him that she was doing him this big favor by going there with her illness and all. She wanted to cancel the trip at the very last minute despite the fact they had planned this trip for months. The only reason he was going there was because she had put that trip on their bucket list of things to do. He kept reminding himself that it was his thousand dollars on the line not hers. If they didn't show up, he would lose his deposit. If she had given him more time, he could have cancelled out without losing his deposit. He was very angry over the whole thing because he wasn't a skier, and they would be inside the cabin all of the time. He was determined to keep it warm and cozy that was the reason for all of the wood. He had very little sympathy over the whole thing.

They finally got to the building where he would check in. She stayed in her SUV. When he got to the counter, there was a woman pleading with the clerk that she wanted to rent a cabin.

"Don't you have any cancellations? I am willing to pay extra for something."

The clerk said, "I'm sorry, nothing is available."

When Michael heard that, he had a big smile on his face. He explained his situation to the lady. Now there were two smiling faces.

"Before I do anything, let me explain everything to my date."

He went back to the SUV.

"There's a woman that wants to buy my tickets. We can go home, and your mother will be happy.   Is that going to suit you?"

It was amazing how quickly the vinegary gaze on her face changed to a smile "No, I want to stay here."

He laughed to himself because he was so used to her manipulations and the way she tried to control things.

"But that's what you were saying all the way up here. You said that you didn't want to be here, and I was saying I didn't want to lose $1,000 but this is a win-win situation."

Now, with all smiles, pleading with him. "No, I want to stay."

He milked it for all it was worth. It was wonderful advantage he had over her. He liked her but wasn't that mad about her, and particularly at this point he was so willing to tell her to jump into the lake.

He smiled. "Okay, if you're sure that's what you want Poppy."

He really wanted to be there. He did feel a little bad having to tell the woman that they decided to stay.

Now, he was back with Poppy, he loved how quickly her mood changed. She was so excited by now. With a smile, from cheek to cheek, she was even willing to help him move the wood and all the other paraphernalia inside of the cabin.

Chapter 14

Settling In

They got to the cabin, and it was a beautiful cabin looking right out on the lake. They were just a few feet from the shore and part of the lake was covered with ice. There was snow all around them. The cabin was quite spacious with a big fireplace, but he noticed that the rug had a few large burnt marks.

He immediately went to work and started up a nice toasty fire as she started to fix up some drinks. They were nice and warm She served the drink laced with brady and lots of honey. The hot drink was good for her pneumonia. He could see now, as she coughed, that she was in some pain. So, she wasn't lying to him.

She had brought all her writings with her. She wanted to reorganize everything and put them in order. There was a little nook near them. They sat there and finally relaxed while drinking their medicinal drinks. As she was going through different poems, occasionally stopping while reading one. As she went along, he admired her poetry they were burning remarks and she had a way with words. He just felt she should be published. He was impressed with her intellect.

Later Poppy fixed meals while he kept the fire going. He was sort of a pyromaniac. As a little boy, he loved playing with matches and fire. He just loved the matches.   They were fantastically big. When you struck them. they created a big flame something he could never duplicate today with our safety matches. They didn't make matches like that anymore.   It was providential that he never burned down his house. One day, a fire he started in the basement got out of hand about twenty feet away from drums of heating oil. The drums would have exploded.   Fortunately, with his help the fire was extinguished.   The next day his grandmother discovered some of the charred remains and decided that she had to do something about it.

She got the basement furnace going with flames almost roaring out of it. She grabbed him and said in Polish. "Look you like the fire so much how about if I put your hands inside of the flame."

He was much more attentive about starting fires, at least not where she could see him.

Poppy looked at him in wonder as he made the fireplace glow and a few times she was afraid.   She told him later.

"You know, I thought you were going to burn the cabin down."

Chapter 15

Time For Some Brewskis And Sex

Poppy liked beer. He was not that much of a beer drinker but when she was with him; he drank beer right along with her. They didn't bring any beer with them so that meant going out in the cold to the local grocery store. It was about 7 or 8 at night, it was freezing out there. He had bought this cotton Jacket that was unique in the way. He was so proud of that coat because it was incredible soft and thick. As he walked down the street to the grocery store, he was warm. To many people this would not be worth mentioning but for a Southern Californian it was a big deal. They hate the cold.

When he got back, she was all smiles and they started to consume the beer and it never took very much to get her buzzed. She was now all bubbly, laughing and having fun, Joyous despite her pneumonia. They went to bed early and they had great sex.

She seemed so happy. Just before they went under. "You know." He said, "When you have a little beer, you're quite a lot of fun."

She looked at him cross-eyed, but it was true; she was in a funky mood until she had a few beers.

He was a incredible snorer. He was so bad that when he was on business trips at a hotel or motel people from the bottom floor would be ringing his room or knocking on his door. They could hear him three floors away. So, the next day, when he awoke, she was already up and ready to leave. She had her sour face look again and he was wondering if she heard him snoring. He never knew whether she did or not. she never told him.

"Was I snoring?   Did I keep you awake? Was everything okay?"

She just kept looking at him with her sour face.

They finally made it back to Fullerton and it was near noon, they headed to their favorite cheap Chinese restaurant. At the end of the meal, she says. "I need $700 from you a month."

That was a bummer. There was no way that he was going to give her $700 a month. He couldn't even believe that she asked him for that. He knew by now that she was a Shopaholic. He knew she made a respectable salary as a nurse.

Chapter 16

Goodbye Andrea And Good Riddance

Andrea finally moved back to Canada. Andrea, he was told, decided to get married. It was at this point that Poppy had totally disowned her. He asked her from time to time.

"Have you heard from Andrea."

He noticed that there was no glitter in her eyes that was there before when Andrea's name was mentioned

As always, she would look straight ahead when she was in this type of mood. But there was that flatness in her tone. She spoke as if she was a robot. She used her lips and tongue as a snake uses its' tongue scenting different odors in the air.

"No, she's not my friend. I'm not interested in her. I lost a lot of respect for her at that party. She's nothing but a slut. Really, the way she wanted those two guys and the way she enjoyed it."

A long time would go by, and he heard nothing about Andrea, and he would have to probe Poppy to get an update.

Of course, he knew what was happening. It was incredible sometimes; he was so tuned into what she was thinking that he understood it all. One of the wonderful aspects of their relationship was their honesty with one another. He didn't want to be misleading about that. It might take some time before everything was on the table but most of time it was instant. She was so complicated, whether she was being double standard, triple standard, quadrupled standard or whatever standard. But the truth always came out

Much later, with a puff and ending in sarcastic tones.

"Now, she is back in Canada, being the perfect Indian Squaw, married and pregnant."

Using her sexy drinking look. "Joe keeps asking me. When are we going to do our threesome again?"

He could understand the way she felt. He was just like her, trust no one, let only a few people into your life and expect loyalty. When you see a person who doesn't have any loyalty, it just hurts. I guess that's why divorces are so rough. You feel like someone took what you considered to be secret and distributed it to the whole wide world. We are always looking for that someone else to fill the one half of ourselves. Having no one --- feels empty.

In the end, he suspected that it was Andrea who got tired of Poppy and not the other way around. It was Poppy's constant hypochondria.

One got tired hearing those chronic health complaints all the time. Hypochondriac's do that to you.

She was always in medical problem or depression and at this moment it was her newfound concern for uterine cancer. Poppy would go on and on. Seeing one doctor after another. She even asked him to accompany her on one of those visits. But in fairness to Poppy, he had been married to a nurse and they are like that, they are hypochondriacs. But again, being abnormal is just shade off from so called normal. And he now believed this was another indication of her borderline personality as well as her noticeable addictive shopping. But he had to remind himself that her chameleon personality was the real marker in this type of neurotic person. We are all neurotics; it only becomes a problem if it interferes with our work or our relationship or with our so-called loved ones.

He would always remind himself what he had learned from his professor at summer school at Trinity College in Hartford Connecticut, it was his first course in psychology.

"Psychosis is a relative thing. A banker always forgetting the combination to the safe because he is having mental problem is different compared to a ditch digger. The banker's problem will really stand out. Mental illness is relative."

Yes, she also had a lot of back pain and constantly complaining. He was sure she was taking her share of medication for that pain. She loved opiates. There was always some medical crisis in her life. It was pneumonia that he had to put up with for three months.

"Ha-ha, I finally got a thousand pills of Valium, I did a good job talking to my doctor and he finally gave them to me."

She took those pills as if they were candy. It was a cute looking pill that were pink and shaped like a valentine heart. She never swallowed them. She simply just placed the pills under her tongue until they dissolved. The first time she did it, he must have had questioning look on his face. She said. " You see, if you put it underneath your tongue; it works a lot faster."

Poppy later admitted. "I think Andrea was questioning me about my cancer."

The wonderful thing about Poppy was she knew she was-- a hypochondriac. And she was telling him that she could understand her problem even though she might not be able to do anything about it. It's the crazy people that don't know that they are crazy. They are the ones you need to worry about. Being crazy from Michael perspective. ("We are all crazy. Look at the world we live in. Think about war.")

The old wives' tale: "If you say you are crazy than you aren't" The fact that Poppy was so intelligent saved her from many missteps. He guessed that's why he found her so intriguing, her sheer mischievous intelligence. It was her intelligence that kept her spinning (spinning in the right way). After all aren't we all moving at the speed of forty-five miles per second through space, on our planet. Yes, spinning from Day to Night, through all different seasons. It is so hard to accept that we see this whole world in our own illusion. Our prospective of a moment, that changes with time.

Even he, with his unflappability, one medical complaint after another starts becoming exhausting. Like the drip, drip of leaky faucet. It was getting to him. He went back and forth in his thoughts, always thinking about her poetry. One of Poppy's poems always floated in his head. He wished he had a better memory or had copies of some of her stuff. He remembered two of them that made him chuckle overtime.

I SWEAR TO TELL THE WHOLE TRUTH

AND NOTHING BUT THE TRUTH

AND A LITTLE WHITE LIE

OUR RELATIONSHIP

IS LIKE MOP AND GLOW

IT JUST

DOESN'T GLOW ANY MORE

Chapter 17

Poppy Just A Little Like Frida Kahlo

He was sure that all her medical problems were not all psychological. He saw how she finally solved her acme problem. He saw what a little flea did to her whole leg. Just thinking about that one flea bite and how black and blue her entire leg looked after just one little flea bite. And now he saw the very positive results when she changed her diet and stayed away from certain foods that the doctor prescribed for her blood type. He also witnessed how quickly she could get drunk on almost one drink. She did have a lot of bodily problems, she was more like, Frida Kahlo, who spent her whole life in pain. They both had their unusual bisexual leaning. And in some fashion, she looked a lot like Frida, that boyish look and maybe even that Native American look. Poppy had told him that she was part Indian. She didn't dress in the Mexican fashion, exactly in the same way Frida did but she did dress in an unusual flair. That is, if and when she decided to get dressed up. Maybe he was stretching that comparison a bit, Poppy never had a steel bar that ran from her vagina and out of her back, as Frida had, from that historical trolley accident. No, she wasn't Frida, who was married to the famous Mexican Painter and a lover of Trotsky.

But really aren't we all in the same boat? Aren't we all talented and unheard of?   How many Van Goths have there been in this world, who have come and gone, never being recognized. For example, he never listened to the young English singer, Amy Winehouse, who died of alcohol poisoning at only twenty-six. It was only after she died that he appreciated her talent. Some people explained this phenomenon of after fame. Those people weren't fully appreciated. They were like fine wine that needed time to mature. He couldn't accept that answer. Why did someone have to become obnoxiously famous before we can appreciate their talent. He saw a future world where a person's talent would be recognized before all that craziness takes over which so often accompanies the process of being famous. Poppy had a lot to show for her life. She touched a lot of people. Oh, if people heard her poems, the way he heard her poems, she would be just as interesting and famous as Frida.

She was getting her last treatments and she wanted to get together with him afterwards. It was convenient for him to just pick her up and drive her to the doctor and then they would go out. When he met her doctor, he was blown away because he had known this gentleman, when the doctor was a simple laboratory technician. Now, he had a PhD. He was a specialist in skin diseases. They both laughed at what a small world it is.

Mark start babbling, proud of what he had achieved.

"I wish I had pictures of her before and after. Doesn't she look one hundred percent better?"

Poppy broke out with her famous smile, hearing the platitudes.

"She has one of those rare blood types. Research has shown us that if we eliminate some of the fatty meats and other ingredients, we can improve a person's skin condition. Obviously, in this case we have shown that it works."

Chapter 18

Poppy And Her Sister Lucy

When he first met Lucy, he was looking for similarities between Poppy and her sister. Something that might be similar in their jaws, noses, bones, ears, cheeks, chins, hair, or smell. He always did that whenever he was introduced to siblings. They had nothing in common except for her sister's thinness and height. Her features did not impress him. In fact, Lucy was extremely unattractive and bordered on ugly. In comparison, Poppy looked beautiful, and we already know that Michael was never impressed with Poppy's facial appearance. Despite what he was feeling, he sensed that Lucy could become an ally. He wanted to know everything he could about Poppy's history.

Sometime later, he needed someone to clean his home. Poppy volunteered her sister. He now had a road to a relationship and understanding of what was going on between Joe, her mother, stepfather, and brother. It ended up that he had many projects for her sister. Besides cleaning he needed to refurbish his kitchen cabinets and change them from mahogany to white. Styles change in ten years, and in those years the style went from white cabinets to dark wood and back to white. She was an excellent worker. She had little employment and he assumed that Poppy was totally responsible for taking care of her. There it was this codependency between her and her sister. There was also something weird between the mother and her children.

One day, while working on the cabinets, she blurted out some interesting information. The expression on Lucy's face looked like someone who had tasted sour milk. As she talked, her remarks seemed to be in disapproval of her sister's actions. She explained to him. "When my sister and I lived together, we had a nice home in Fullerton. She had a boyfriend that when payday came, he would give her his complete check. They were in all kinds of freaky sex. I think he liked bondage."

Michael later was able to bring up the matter about Poppy living with her sister in their home in Fullerton.

" You know what he went and did? I had some pictures that we took together, and I told him I didn't want anyone to have them. I just threw them out. He had found all those pictures and kept them and that was just a No-No. He just had to go after that."

He liked' taking pictures, but he noticed how hypersensitive she was whenever he tried to photograph her. She always had that secretive quality. He suspected that had something to do with her borderline personality. She was just very secretive, and it bordered on paranoia.

Chapter 19

Poppy And Her Sister

Surprise!!! Lunch with Poppy. He didn't understand how this upcoming **EVENT** happened. And it was an event with a capital E. She lived by one of those crazy night schedules, working twelve-hour night shifts and then once she was finished, sleeping most of the time, through lunch time, especially lunch time.

She would often remind him. "I just love working those hours, because I can get four days off in row."

The restaurant they were going to meet at was in Fullerton, (You know, Poppy's love for Fullerton). In fact, the restaurant was only a mile from where she lived. This place where they would eat today would become their favorite Chinese restaurant. It was sort of a hole in the wall, but their food was excellent. Okay, cheap, too.

He had many lunch meetings there before, when he worked at NTS, which was just a block away. There were lots of good memories that he associated with this restaurant. Being there today, brought back all those wonderful experiences, having lunch with his partner, a world renown Hungarian Scientist. They both were rebels and always had comments about the stupidity of the company. Lunch hours were ideal to vent on all those stupid company's practices. The company had no real understanding of their business, the remediation of hazard materials. The company's decisions to be in that market were based on textbooks that were outdated. For example, they thought that they could charge thousands of dollars per ton for recycled clean soil when in fact the price had fallen to hundreds of dollars.

Today, for some reason, she invited her sister, and he was sort of excited about that. It would be another opportunity to allow him to get more insight into Poppy's childhood. At least, that was what he was thinking. He loved gossip. And he might even learn more about her policeman, Joe from gossip slips that her sister might make. He might even get more information about her other affairs.

He also felt sort of honored by this gesture of letting him have a meeting with her sister because Poppy was so private, in her way, she was sharing her family with him. He took this gesture as her trust in him.

Back to her sister. He knew that they had the same mother but different fathers. He knew this already from stuff that Poppy had shared with him. Her mother was once married to a wealthy Hawaiian when Lucy was young. Lucy was now twenty-seven, compared to Poppy, who was now forty years old. Poppy looked only a little older than her sister. She also used all that lingo and mannerism of a younger woman which added to her appearance of being youthful.

He really couldn't understand why, but he knew that for some reason Poppy felt that she had a kind of motherly type of responsibility for her sister. Poppy labeled her behavior as codependency. Lucy had Muscular Dystrophy and the doctors used implanted electrodes to help Lucy with her movements. But to hear the way Poppy talked about her sister; it seemed like Lucy was a sick cookie both physically as well as mentally. She had characteristics that he liked which was a little bit childish, and very honest. He didn't see anything particularly unusual about her. There was the one time when he and Poppy visited Lucy's apartment. He got the tour. She was very proud of her bedroom. And there was good reason for that. Lucy had a collection of at least fifteen almost life-size dolls in that room. He did think that was rather strange.

He remembered how he felt and probably had a strange expression on his face.

She explained. "They are beautiful, aren't they? See those eyes, they cost hundreds of dollars."

"Yes, they look as if they are looking straight at me. And the colors of those eyes look so real."

She proudly pointed out. "Look how real those arms look. And those dresses cost hundreds of dollars. She pointed to the dolls in the corner of the room. "I made those dresses by myself."

She went on and on and on. Wow, she was a collector just like her sister. He thought that it was kind of weird. He knew that Lucy was on disability, and he could see those dolls weren't cheap.

His eyes were exploding in disbelief.

"If you don't believe me, you can check it all out at my hobby shop in Garden Grove.

He did think that all those dolls in her bedroom was a bit much. He had to question Poppy.

"Poppy, your sister's collection has to be a very expensive hobby?"

Poppy just rolled her eyes.

"Do you know what my precious little sister did? She needed some more money for her doll hobby; she went directly to Joe and asked if she could borrow some money from him without even asking me. Joe being the nice guy that he is, gave it to her. I told him not to expect her to pay him back. Joe didn't care; he was just happy that he could do something nice for my sister."

He thought to himself, that Joe was a nice guy. He knew that he would never be that generous. Something that Poppy never quite said to him, but he felt it, that he could never compete with Joe when it came to handouts. It seemed Joe made a good amount of money as compared to what he did. It wasn't that he didn't make a good living but after refinancing his home many times over, his mortgage was very high. After all he lived in Huntington Beach and close to the ocean and that property wasn't cheap. Besides Joe never went through a divorce, his wife committed suicide by jumping off the roof of their home. And let's face it, Michael just wasn't the generous type of person. What was his was his.

But, just out of curiosity, he did go to the hobby store. He got the address of that hobby shop from Lucy. The store was a strange place to visit. On the shelves, were hundreds of artificial eyes in all different colors, staring right at him. They all looked real and spooky. That's when he found out that her dolls were expensive, close to a thousand dollars apiece.

Chapter 20

Lunch And The Cold Shoulder From Poppy

He parked his car and with extra energy that he didn't know he had; he opened the door of the restaurant. He saw them in the corner sitting in a large booth, Poppy on one end and the sister on the opposite end. they were into something he thought was rather intense. As he walked toward the table, he could almost feel a negative cloud hanging over them. It reminded him of the *Little Abner Fosdick Cartoon*. He loved devouring it in the Sunday Comic Section of the newspaper. It was a character who walked with a black cloud over his head and wherever he went, the cloud followed him with rain, thunder, and all. At least that's what he remembered. That's the way he felt at that very moment. He just didn't know if the cloud was over Poppy's head or over her sister's head.

As he approached, Poppy seemed menacing and vicious. He had experienced her menacing mood before after their wonderful night together at Big Bear. It was then when she asked him to give her several hundred dollars a month. Her mood, he was sure had something to do with her finances. He sat down surrounded with this feeling of being unwelcomed. He sat on the same side of the table where her sister was so that Poppy sat at the opposite end. It gave the appearance that she was the judge sitting opposite two plaintiffs. She wasn't courteous towards him, and she was very snappy. He couldn't quite understand what message she was trying to send. He felt she wanted her sister to think that he really meant nothing to her. There was no conversation, no small talk. and now he wasn't even sure why he was there.

He was feeling more like a Boy Scout who had a small twig smoldering after focusing light through a magnifying glass, blowing on it to get the fire going. He sat there with her sister and talking in somewhat a manic mood trying to keep a conversation in play. After he finished, rushing through his meal; he grabbed the check. The goodbyes were brisk. He was a little bit disappointed and angry, but he understood the pattern. She wanted everyone to know that she was the boss and if they wanted to play with her then they would have to play by the rules, her rules. Afterall, in her head, she was running a business and she was a businesswoman. He had to remind himself that she had been a prostitute and money was always in play.

Yes, he did walk away feeling hurt and angry, but he understood the dynamics of what was going on and it was very complicated. He tried not to take it personally, although part of him did. The relationship in his mind was winding down because five years ago none of this would have bothered him. Poppy had continually told him that she was co-dependent, and he had thought it only concerned her mother, but he could see how her sister was also involved. Watching the scene with her sister, he understood what she was talking about. He had assumed that this conversation with her sister was concerning money. He was now able to fit the pieces together and that moodiness occurred when Poppy needed additional money. He understood why Lucy came to her and asked her for money because she thought Poppy had money or could get money. In the past she was able to fill Poppy with guilt and in that way, she always got help from Poppy.

He really didn't understand why he was invited to their luncheon. Obviously one of her motivations was for him to pick up the bill. She was always busy, and it was a moment that she could squeeze him in. He had assumed that in the past, Poppy had looked to him for relief from her anxiety. Poppy probably felt that this meeting with her sister was going to be confrontational and therefore he was invited to act as a buffer. He knew the anger was not directed at him. What happened today was not a good sign. It really showed a lack of respect.

He was always a dreamer yet today he had to accept reality. When he first met Poppy, she said let's hang out together and he should have kept it at that level. He understood that it was a couple's society and he accepted that. He wasn't sure at this point that either he or Poppy worked well with other people especially in a romantic arrangement. It was fortunate for him that she wasn't a knockout beauty like his mother. He seemed be infatuated with women that looked like his mother and then he would have been putty in their hands. He sensed that this breakup when it came would never be painful. For some reason with Poppy, it was like he had been given a vaccine and therefore the bug wasn't as damaging as it could have been. In all relationships, two people grow together or they grow apart. He accepted the fact that she was smarter than he was, that she was more experienced in the world. He could feel as the weeks went by a decision would be made. He knew that she was drawn to him for whatever reason but like all relationships a moment of change must occur. In the process of that change someone might have to be excluded. In this society, there must be a winner and there must be a loser. As he learned in research, even rhesus monkeys had a hierarchy. There was a leader and a lieutenant, and someone was always on the bottom. The odd thing about the monkey hierarchy, a weak lieutenant usually ended up at the bottom and not at the top.

As time went on, he would experience more and more of the shifting of the sand. After this lunch, he was getting the where-with-all to see the illusion of the relationship and his dreamy aspects of what would happen if he married her. He had to accept the fact that she was fickle. He knew that her fickleness came from her feelings of abandonment. There was a tendency to destroy a relationship. It was the, I Love You, Hate You Syndrome.

Women like Poppy can play on your illusions. Life is a dance, fortunately or unfortunately, you can become satiated and want to move on to something new and different, yet he marveled as he was getting older that he seemed not to like change. He watched his cat desire a certain food and never seem to deviate from that one ideal brand. He saw it with Poppy and himself. They would repeatedly frequent just a few restaurants. Yes, they were all creatures of habit and as one got older; the habits become more restrictive. Yet in the beginning that was what was so attractive about being with younger person. In the beginning, that's why he was so attracted to Poppy, she was so open to new ideas and things to do.

Chapter 21

Girls' Night Out

Meeting Ashley The Twenty-four Year Old Stripper

Looking down from the stage into the audience, she saw a woman immaculately attired in very dressy black lacy evening outfit. She was sitting at a table all by herself and drinking a beer out of a bottle.

Ashley had to move her eyes from person to person as she performed, a technique that she used to make the audience believe that she was looking at them. Yet, she found herself being drawn to this woman. The way she held the bottle and then slowly sipping her beer. It was unusual and somewhat seductive. This woman looked sad as if she had been stood up on a very important date. There was gloom about her. Her physical appearance was very unusual. She had high cheekbones, dark brown hair, and a dark complexion. She had features of American Indian. She had a boyish unisex appearance and yet seemed very feminine dressed in her expensive attire. She had a nice slender figure and seemed to be five feet seven about her own height. She looked so out of place in this bar. She could feel her eyes studying every part of her in such a forceful way. She knew now that this woman wanted to make love with her.

When her dance was over, she didn't make her typical rounds but walked directly over to her table. "You look very beautiful in that dress yet so depressed. Were you stood up? Are you alright?"

Poppy smiled her whimsical smile. Spoke to her in a control voice. "No, girls' night out."

Ashley looked to see if she had a ring on her finger, but she had no rings on either hand. In fact, she had no jewelry, at all. She didn't even have earrings.

" A friend told me about this place and I decided I needed a beer. I enjoyed your dancing."

Ashley smiled at her compliment sensing the subtle undertone in Poppy's voice.

"Oh, I do this for fun. I'm really a paralegal soon to be a lawyer. The lawyers examine is next week and I'm positive I'll pass on my first try. This place is good for me. It helps me forget the gloom of the courtroom."

She stuck her hand out in business kind of way. "My name is Ashley."

With a twinkle in her eye, knowing now that she had a victim. Poppy giggled. "My name is Poppy. It's a nickname my sister gave to me when I was young. I think she got confused and meant to call me Peppy. I liked it and preferred it over my real name."

Ashley was also sure of what was happening and somewhat excited about her prospects. She went to the next step. "Do you live around here?"

Poppy jumped on the question acknowledging the nonverbal invitation and said. " I live just a few blocks from here. That's why I came here. I don't have to worry about driving too far to get home." Poppy gave her all knowing smile again. "Don't want to get caught drinking and driving"

"What a coincidence, I live around here too. I like to talk with you some more, but I must get ready for my next number. I have one more set then I will be done. We can go over to my place. I think I have just the thing to cheer you up."

She held Poppy's hand. "Will you wait for me?"

Poppy held her hand and gave her a typical intense look that communicated the answer very unmistakably. There was no question in Ashley's mind what that intense look meant. She felt her body shake in anticipation. This lady was no novice. Poppy's eyes had a very dark look but at just that moment they cleared with the look of the vulnerability of a young girl.

Ashley was finishing out for the night, so she decided to be riskier in what she normally did in her act. She was not afraid to bear her all and she wanted Poppy to get a good look. She had already concluded that Poppy was bisexual, and she found this woman attractive. Poppy had a certain masculinity yet hidden in softness. She didn't seem to be a very attractive female at least not by her standards but then this was better for her. She always enjoyed being the better-looking one and she was. She knew she was all female. This was acknowledged every night by all the cheers she got every time she performed. She knew that her breasts were voluptuous even if she had aid from a well-known plastic surgeon. She had a perfect figure with legs to match. Her hair was light brown and long and fine. She wasn't sure how old Poppy was but obviously older than her own twenty-four years. It was really hard to guess but she guessed she could be in her 30's but very early 30's. She knew what aging could do to a woman. After all she associated with only the finest of women. Her newest friend Susie, a judge, had to be in her late fifties. Poppy didn't have any of telltale signs of crowfeet or wrinkles and the skin around her neck was tight.   She liked her sureness, assertiveness, and her sense of humor.   She saw that Poppy had a bite and hardness with just a touch of vulnerability. She seemed to be like herself, someone who would never leave any stones unturned. She also decided that like her she was not that impressed with men.   If she was then, Poppy wouldn't be here watching her strip. Ashley preferred the company of another woman. It was easier to discuss things with another woman. Everything was more comfortable. There were fewer pretenses that were so necessary with men. They always wanted something. Women were less demanding. She realized that men were more powerful, and she enjoyed learning from them their way of creating the energy that was needed to compete. She liked the feeling of a father like figure who would be there to protect her if everything came tumbling down. In fact, she had a great father, she did love him. He had given her everything she needed.

She knew she was young, bright, and beautiful. She didn't need to work in this sleazy club. She didn't need the money, but she was proud that her nude body could draw so much attention. The forty thousand dollars tax free dollars she earned wasn't something to sweat at either. It was thrilling to see men and women drooling over her. Now, she had found a new friend and she knew that this little creature needed a helping hand

Poppy by now couldn't get enough of Ashley and she knew that Ashley was impressed with her, too. She had slipped out with her real name and given her far more information about herself than would have been necessary. She was a little surprised in Ashley invite but obviously she was a woman who knew what she wanted.

Poppy sat and admired Ashley's body and her gyrations. Poppy knew what it was like to work in a place like this and she knew that Ashley like herself preferred women. She was acquainted with the procedure. It was typical to throw up money on the stage or personally put it into the bikini while she still had her bikini on. She folded up $100.00 bill and went slowly and deliberately to the stage.   Of course, all the men had their eyes on Poppy as she purposefully enjoyed her own moment in the limelight and quite aware of the commotions she was orchestrating. When she placed the bill in Ashley's bikini the crowd all applauded, hooting, and howling.

Poppy gently placed the folded one-hundred-dollar bill and placed it into the side of Ashley's bikini and she smiled with her knowing look and then slowly walked back to her table.

That money and Poppy, inspired Ashley to new heights. She could see the Ben Franklin on the bill. She decided to pull it out and unfold it. She wanted to let the audience see that it was a one-hundred-dollar bill. She ran the bill from her front bottom and slowly over the rest of her body and then kissed it.

She now really kicked into her act. Poppy was mesmerized and marveled at the way she lowered herself down the pole. She was aroused and lusted and wanted to stroke her strong legs and wonderfully proportioned buttocks. She felt stirred but Poppy was an artist of looking detached and not aroused.

Chapter 22

Good Drugs And Good Sex

Ashley place was easy to get to. It was a nice little home and in a very respectful neighborhood.

They ended up in the kitchen. "I told you I had something better than a drink at my place. I think this stuff will cheer you up."

Ashley reached into one of the kitchen cabinets and pulled out a little vial which was hidden behind some coffee cups. It was a vial filled with white powdery coke. With a big grin on her face, she showed it off the Poppy.

"You're okay with coke?"

Poppy laughed. "My favorite stuff is heroin. But I have never turned down a few lines of that stuff."

"Heroin? Well, I got some stuff in my bedroom which is almost as good. I only share it with special friends. Are you going to become one of my special friends?"

"I am here, aren't I?"

"Yes, I guess, I 've caught you in my little spiderweb."

She paused as she poured some of the white stuff on her mirror-like kitchen granite countertop. After reaching into another drawer, she pulled out a small knife and made several nice lines of the white powder.

Next, she handed Poppy a small tube of glass that was in the same drawer. "You're my guest."

Without missing a beat, Poppy in all her sexual grace quickly snorted up two lines.

"What do you think? --- good stuff, hah? This is pure stuff, I got it from one of the DA's friends. They got it from the police department, from some confiscated stuff."

"Poppy in her low husky sexy voice said. "Honey, this is exactly what I needed."

While Ashley was taking her turn. Poppy picked up a large wooden spatula that was sitting on the counter. While Ashley was still bent over, Poppy place one hand on Ashley's behind.

"You have such a pretty ass. I remembered how great it looked when you were on that stage."

With that spatula, she whacked her behind, several times, as hard as she could.

"I want you to strip down for me. Give me, your little dance, just as you did tonight. Just as you did in front of the whole audience of men that were there."

Poppy then forcefully turned her around and grabbed her and gave her a strong kiss. While they kissed, they both started to rip at the other's clothes. Now both were on the floor moving in and out of each other. Ashley suddenly got up and grabbed Poppy's hand to lift her up.

"Let's go into the bedroom. I got some real good stuff in there, just for you. I got some opium powder, really great stuff."

Laughing and giggling, they were both off to the bedroom.

"Don't I have a great bedroom?"

She pulled open a drawer from her nightstand.

"I love this stuff but use it on only special occasions and I feel this is hell of a special occasion."

She pulled out a big powder puff smacked it on Poppy's face and then her own. "I find this is the easiest way to use it. Take a deep breath. Do you feel it? Isn't it great?"

From that time on all you could hear is a lot of heavy breathing and sighing. "Poppy, I have never experienced anything like this before. You are really good. You are one of a kind. I like what you are doing to me. I like what I am feeling."

From time to time, Poppy would roll her over and grab her behind and totally dominate her. Poppy could feel how soft her skin felt underneath her hand. The beautiful skin of a young woman in her prime. There was no jiggle of fat nothing but solid muscle.

Ashley could feel what she was thinking. "That another reason, why I do the stripping thing. It's good for my body. All that exercise. That's my gym time."

Ashley was squirming. Poppy had all three of her fingers inserted deeply inside of Ashley and moving her hand and pushing inside of her as fast as she could. That was Poppy's trademark, lots of unbelievable energy.

"Don't stop! Oh Lord, forgive me. Such pleasure. I am almost there. Please! Please! don't stop!"

Poppy was also breathing hard and in her low gasping trademark dreamy seductive voice. "Go ahead Honey, you earned it, you worked hard for it."

Poppy's encouraging words were slow now trying to catch her breath. She loved conquering and she was just as excited. And she was working hard pounding Ashley with now four fingers moving in and out of her while at the same time sucking vigorously on her breast. Then gasping for breath and speaking from time to time between it all

"Showing off your beautiful young body--- to that whole place--- all those strangers. --- All of them, just wanting to fuck you----------------- that must make you feel so great."

Ashley now in total delirium. "Yes, I am superwoman. Oh God, yes, I am. I can feel everything."

(All those drugs were working well on both of them. You can't beat first grade drugs.)

Feeling her conquest, controlling someone else, Poppy could feel that she herself was super wet. As she was sucking Ashley's tit and knowing that Ashley's was ready for her orgasm, Poppy bit her nipple hard and with her other hand like a gymnastic pushed her finger up Ashley's ass.

For a moment Ashley lost all her identity. It was like something like from her dreams as little girl free from gravity. She was flying. She remembered an article where you could fly on one of the moons of either Jupiter or Saturn. That moon had an atmosphere that was so heavy that a human could fly. And right now, she was flying and floating.

As Ashley was having her many small multiple climaxes, Poppy turned around and placed her bottom part near Ashley. Still consumed in her delirious heat, Ashley started kissing Poppy on the middle of Poppy's thigh. She kept kissing Poppy until she could taste Poppy's wetness as she reached her engorged labia and throbbing clit, and licked Poppy as vigorously as she could.

It wasn't very long before Poppy was shaking uncontrollably and yelling. "FUCK! FUCK! FUCK!"

Chapter 23

Ashley Likes Poppy

Please Move In With Me

Light was coming through the window, when Ashley explained that she was studying hard and ready to take her bar exam the next month. She explained that she was only twenty-four years old and wanted to have fun before she would become a lawyer. She was doing the stripping for diversion. Her father was very proud of her and loved spoiling her. He had purchased the home for her. He lived back East, so she had the whole place to herself; in fact, she wanted to know if Poppy would be interested in moving in with her.

As they were saying their goodbyes and walking toward the door. Ashley opened one of the bedroom doors

It was a fully equipped dungeon. She saw the bars on the ceiling for hanging people in different positions She saw rows of different spanking tools:

Canes, switches, mask and many strap on dildoes.

Ashley pointed to the strap- on. "I am sure next time you will want to fuck me in booth of my holes."

Poppy just grinned. "Well at least you know what's in store for you!"

Even though Ashley was a strong woman, she just loved the effect Poppy had on her. She didn't mind being submissive to Poppy

In a very submissive tone. "I have never had anyone that pleased me as you have."

"I am not surprised; they tell me that once someone has me that they never can go back to simple whatever."

"Would you consider moving in with me. You won't have to pay for anything."

Poppy was surprised she didn't expect that.

"Seriously, I would love to have you as a roommate. This place gets pretty lonely when you are by yourself."

Poppy hesitated. "WOW, what a great offer. But the lady that I live with."

Ashley picked it up. "She would be upset."

"She's more like a mother to me and she's very vanilla. She's very fragile and I almost think she would die without me."

Poppy smiled. "But honey that won't affect our life together. I would love to move in but give me some time with my friend. She needs me and I don't want her to feel as if I am going to dump her. You understand?"

"I Just want you to understand how I feel about you."

"I know and that is so sweet. I feel the same way towards you. I don't need to tell you. I have been around the block a few times. But that's a story for another time."

Michael later got all the fine details from Poppy.   She had that sheepish smile on her face when she said.

"Can you imagine she wanted me to move in with her. She really liked me. She is beautiful and she's only in her early twenties and smart.   She's going to take the bar exam."

"I know some guys must take it more than once."

"Oh, not her, she'll pass it on her first try. she's so clever."

"Well, are you going to move in with her?"

He already knew her answer and that would be just another confirmation that something existed between her and Shirley.

"I can't. I don't want to lose my Independence."

"Well, at least you have another friend. I like to see what she looks like; she sounds quite interesting."

"You would love this. You know she even has a dungeon set up in one of her bedrooms. It's fully equipped. She seems to have everything in terms of sexual gadgets.   She's going to invite me to some of her parties. She is very well connected with other lawyers and even some judges and of course politicians."

"You sure have a knack of connecting with people."

Chapter 24

Here's The Deal

I Want Sex My Way

He was trying to figure out a way to broaden their sexual experiences. Somehow, he was happy to know that he could never be like Poppy, but it was fun shirting the edges with her. He just wanted to be himself; whoever that might be. He felt that he was experimental, but he realized he could never let go of his conservative upbringing and he was happy having that assurance. He felt very safe when he was with Poppy; she understood his boundaries or limits. And let's face it he enjoyed his voyeurism; maybe, voyeurism was the wrong word, vicariousness would probably be a better word. He enjoyed some of the experiences that she would share with him.

Now, they were at their favorite PIZZA place, far away from the crowd, in their typical corner booth. They had already finished their first pitcher of beer and were halfway through their second pitcher. They had pretty much finished dissecting the foreign movie, subtitles, and all, that they just finished watching at their favorite foreign movie theater. It was one his favorite things he loved doing with Poppy, because she was always able to express her novel spin on all the movies that they saw together.

"You know, I was thinking that after our trip to Big Bear and you mentioned you wanted me to give you $700 a month. I really felt that was sort of a slap in the face. In fact, I couldn't understand where you were coming from. But I know how you always need money for your different projects. I have been thinking about that and I can afford only four hundred dollars."

He paused, something he had to learn the hard way to do. As salesman, he always wanted to keep talking but he finally learned to shut his mouth and wait. He could feel her gears going. He knew that in her mind, with this carrot, something was happening. She probably saw a new dress or something else on her list of the day.

Now, he was ready.

"But for that four hundred, I want to be able to have what I want from you, just for one evening."

He saw the smile that came over her face. He knew that she saw it as a win-win situation. Somehow, sex connected to money excited her and the process of having the man give up his precious dollars, so that he might have her. It built up her self-esteem. She was never deficient in asking for the money. All prostitutes are interested in getting the money. They made some of the best businessmen. They weren't afraid to close the deal and ask the person to sign on the dotted line.

She was almost laughing. "Why not. To our next get together."

She held up her mug and clinked his.

Chapter 25

The Sex Store And Lots Of Toys

He was fortunate; He was able to assemble a very good collection of sexual paraphernalia. He was so grateful to that X-Rated shop that was right next to Cal. State Fullerton. It was a high-class porn shop, one of a kind in Orange County. They had a large assortment of greeting cards, placards, triple X magazines, a large collection of expensive books on sex. The cliental there were more sophisticated. He was successful when he left his books there, on consignment, and all his books sold well.

It was like having a newspaper route. And you wanted to have your newspapers machine always full. It took a bit of work to stay on top of what was moving, because you never wanted that bin to go down to empty. The books moved quickly but in somewhat regular pattern; he was always on top of it. He never let it go down to having one book or no books. During a period of two months, he found that eight books were the perfect number and that was eighty dollars in merchandise for him.

The agreement he made with the owner, he would leave ten books and when those books moved off the shelves; he would replace them with ten more. He would then use those dollars to purchase merchandise at a big discount.   Because he didn't think of it as being real money, he bought gadgets that were extreme for his taste but looked interesting with possibilities for use in the future. There was always new stuff to purchase. He bought stuff that he didn't need right away. There were items like a leather hood or high duty whip. There were whips of all sorts made of various material. Of course, anything made of leather was four times the price of something not made of leather. It was well stocked, almost as good as Stock Room or Adam and Eve. They had all kinds of S&M costumes, corsets, harnesses, lubricants. edibles, chastity belts, cock harnesses, all sizes, shapes, colors dildos, strap on dildos, clubs, butt plugs, ball stretchers, nipple clamps, and all types of vibrators.

Chapter 26

The Planning For A Night Of Pleasure

He was going to use every angle to get his four hundred bucks worth. He started to spend days in his preparations. Someone, who might have visited him in those days, during this organization, would think that a lunatic lived there. He had all of drawers open, all the closets open, every box, every hiding place, and every conceivable place that some sexual toy might be hidden. He found a lot of stuff that he had forgotten. Stuff that he hadn't seen in years.

He noticed that in one of the Chester drawers, where he stored some his stuff, the drawer was made of artificial wood, glued together with lots of epoxy. Over the years, the latex gadgets dissolved into blobs of black gooey stuff from the unseen solvent (the glue) that was slowly seeping out through the years. Some of that gooey stuff got on and ruined his special collection of different negligees that he collected for women visitors. He was proud of his collection. But the only thing, he was able to save was a full black corset type that pushed up on the women's boobs to make them look bigger. It also had an attachment on the bottom of the corset for stockings. He had another outfit that was made of leather that was a miniskirt. It had a full front with the back opening that displayed full view of a lady's ass and pushed up on her buns. He had all kinds of stockings, super spiked high heels, and even different wigs. In the past, he had developed that healthy sexual spirit via Jessica. She was an Aries, and he was too. She liked to experiment and used dirty words in a seductive way. Jessica was very intelligent, hot, and fiery, and all the things that you would want a woman to be, plus a snapping tight pussy. She liked sex as much as he did and most likely a nymphomaniac. She was one of the few women from the past that he really missed.

Chapter 27

Let's See How Far We Can Go

It was a new day; he was ready to see if his experiment would work. It was now several hours before her arrival. A lot of what he had in mind for the evening was sort of storyboarded in his head. He had a lot of fantasies going on in there. He knew Poppy was so good at what she did.   She was such a chameleon, so capable of harvesting the spirit of the other person.

Everything was ready for their little party. His renters were gone, and he had the whole place to himself. He laid out all the sexual paraphernalia so that the whole lot was easy to get to. He had all the candles that he owned fired up and the lighting adjusted for the proper ambience. He even had the air filled with the sweet aroma of incense. The stereo playing smooth music, Chopin, Jazz and Saida (*Smooth Operator*).

She arrived a little bit earlier than expected but that was fine. She was always on time, and he was ready for her. She was well-dressed, which was sort of unusual. She liked wearing baggie gym pants, no makeup and only neutral colors and glossy lipstick. She had a habit of repeatedly using her glossy lipstick while she talked. Always acting as if her lips were dry.

They were quick to get into the kitchen and then exchange a few kisses. She seemed to be in a great mood, somewhat unusual for her. When he saw the big smile on her face, He had to think to himself that's the difference a few dollars make.

She was excited. "Look what I brought you."

She handed him a grocery bag. He opened the bag and found a large chunk of beef. It was her usual habit, there was a good butcher shop on her way to his place and she would from time present him with a good cut of steak. He was always pleased with this sweet offer.

She sat down at the table and looked relaxed. He immediately gave her a bottle of beer. She had a special way of dramatically holding the bottle gingerly by its' neck as if she was holding a penis. He assumed she had learned to do that for the effect. As she sipped her beer, she seemed wonderfully relaxed and happy. He drank his glass of wine while talking and doing the cooking. She particularly liked loads of onions on her steak, so he was teary eyed as he sliced away. She liked her steak cooked in just a particular manner, which he became adept at doing. It was a beautiful steak something that he would never spend his money on, he was just too frugal; but she was always extravagant, when she was in her element.

Many glasses of wine, many bottles beer, and multiple hits of marijuana later; they found the bedroom. They were both in a great mood. She could see that everything was laid out for her to study and there was a lot of things to look at. He gave her some time to take it all in. He had a costume for himself. He showed her his little outfit. He was trying to be jovial about it, but at this point, he was a little self-conscious.

While she was studying everything, he went into the bathroom to undress and put on this macho leather outfit. He ordered this thing via a catalogue, and it was very new to him. It had multiple leather straps that crisscrossed the top of his body. It all seemed to function for one reason only, in that it was to hold up a little pouch for his private parts. He had some problems because there were so many leather straps. He had practiced before. Once he got it on, he didn't feel that stupid about it. The costume made him feel sexy. One of his ladies that he experimented with; she told him that she came off when she smelled leather. Just thinking of leather got her high. He was hoping that tonight, with all this leather, that he was wearing. He was hoping that it would have the same effect on Poppy.

He was a little excited. It wasn't that easy to get everything properly lined up. She finally helped him get the straps around his shoulders and across the chest and ending up with that little pouch covering his private parts,

"Well, how do I look? Do I look sexy?"

She had a huge smirking smile on her face than with her beautiful sexy bedroom tone. "Yes, very, very sexy."

He helped her to get undressed. With her clothes off, she had a nice figure. She didn't have a body that he would die for. Wendy, his most recent ex-girlfriend, had a perfect muscular exotic figure. Something you would expect from someone who went to the gym every freaking day. What was nice about Poppy's figure was that she didn't have an ounce of fat and everything about her was in perfect proportions. And she looked young.

"I like to try this gag on you."

Almost absent minded, "Oh, before that, I need to put this nice strong leather collar around your neck."

It was an expensive leather collar with several straps on the backside where he could, using real padlocks secure the collar around her neck. Those padlocks added to the bondage features. He had two little locks that he inserted into the rings of the claps and closed them. The front of the collars had a large ring where he was able to attach a leash that he used for his cat.

After he got the whole thing on her. He pulled on the leash. "Is that comfortable for you?"

She nodded.

"By the way, these are the keys."

He had placed them on a separate keychain because they were small, and he didn't want to lose them. The collar was also expensive. If he couldn't open the locks, he had a problem. if that happened, he had no idea what he would do. The collar was made of very thick leather and was almost impossible to cut through it. He would have to, in some way cut it off. Of course, he didn't want to have to do that. He didn't want to destroy this very expensive thick leather collar.

"I am putting the keys over here next to this jar. I might forget where they are, knowing how absent minded I get when I smoke marijuana. I want to be able to open those locks when we are all done playing around. Unless you want to go home wearing it?"

He laughed. "Imagine, what would Shirley say if you came home wearing that collar?"

Poppy could be rather loud when she had her orgasm, and she had a habit of screaming out.

"Fuck, Fuck, Fuck". She was so loud that one his neighbors asked his roommate.

"What's all that screaming about?"

With a smile on his face, his renter reply. "You don't want to know."

He reached for something. He was ready to insert the gag. Then he opened her mouth and inserted a flat rubber balloon like object into her mouth. It was fastened to a small leather belt that he tied up and buckled behind her head. The balloon had a tube that projected out of her mouth and at the other end of the tube was an air pump. It looked like it belonged to a doctor's air pump that is attached to a blood pressure cuff or siphonometer. This black oval elongated pump ball dangled down to around the middle of her chest. As she moved, the ball bounced from one nipple to the next which was stimulating for her and for him, too. He watched the way she squirmed in a kind of pleasure. She looked rather odd with this contraption in her mouth which for some reason excited him.

He grabbed the pump in his hand. It didn't take long to inflate the balloon.

"I know you think that I want you to have all of your freedom to do what you want to do. And you think that I don't want to possess you, but that exactly what I want to do. I want to own you and have you become my slave."

As he was talking, he pumped up the balloon until it filled the inside of her mouth.

"You are always teasing me that you like sucking on a big tit. Well now, this thing is filling all of the inside of your mouth. Now, you have real treat, a whopping tit to suck on."

The beauty of this gadget was not only did it fill up your mouth but not a sound could be heard. She could scream as loud as she wanted and there would be nothing. It was also freeing to know that no matter what you said in your moment of pleasure; no one could hear you, not even yourself. He knew that from personal experience that when he was excited, he made some weird sounds. Even to the point of talking in strange language or as some people would say speaking in tongues. With that gag on, you can say all kinds of crazy stuff, and no one would hear you.

He reached down to play with her clitoris, and he wasn't disappointed. He always loved it when she honored him this way. When she was excited, her fluids would gurgle out of her. As he expected, she was getting slippery, and her clitoris was engorged and sensitive to his slightest touch. Her clit was throbbing, and he felt the continuous gentle flow of her secretions. He was always surprised by her musty smell, something more masculine not the sweet smell that he was used to. Maybe, that was another reason why she was bisexual. She had a different chemistry from other women.

"Yes, I want you to be hot like this, all of the time and I want you to pretend that I am a Sultan and I have a large harem. You can screw as many girls as you want in my harem but understand that you must please only one person and that's me. If you don't, I could have you killed. And if you are obedient and please me, I might even let you fuck one of my eunuchs while I watch you. Knowing what a slut you are. You would thrive in that environment. I know you so well

He had one more thing to do. He reached out for his gadgets and found a small butt plug.

As he slowly inserted it. It went in nice and easy, as she shook a little.

"I just want to make sure that this area is also taken care of before we get started."

He helped her to the end of the bed.

"Why don't you get to the very end of the bed with your fanny sticking up so you are in a better angle for what I need to do next."

He arranged several pillows for her, so she was comfortable. Now that he had her in the right position.

"Well, what should we use here the paddle, the whip, the strap?"

He decided to just start with a plane old strap. As he whipped her with this leather strap, he was amazed. When she was in this state, she thrived on pain. She loved being strapped. She loved playing this role. He would never meet anyone who could take so much punishment and then ask for more.

He continued to coax her. "I want you so well trained that all I have to do is snap my fingers and you would do anything I ask you to do."

He decided to change the pace and use a paddle. She seemed to prefer the flat paddle and he gave her some quick sharp slaps.

"Do you understand?"

She nodded her head. He turned her around so he could look into her eyes. Now using a whip. He slapped the whip across the front of her breast. She couldn't help but blink her eyes. He knew she felt that.

"You always agree but you forget what you agreed to do. What am I to do with you? You tell me what you want me to hear and as soon as I give you some freedom you go back to your own disobedient self."

When he finally finished lashing her front, fanny, and her back they were all rather red from all his effort.

He ran his hand over her.

"You are nice and red now."

He laid her on her back side, flat on the bed. His bed didn't have any post, but he owned special strap contraption that fit under the mattress then folded out on the top of the mattress. It had four ends that allowed a person to be tied down. He decided to try something different. He finally pulled out two sets of handcuffs. "I'm going to have you here, all the way at the top of the bed. Let me get this hand and lock it in."

He finished with her other hand. "Now, I want you to spread your legs so I can get at your private parts shooting out. Just in case should anyone come into the room; they can see just how wet you are. Too bad my renters aren't here; I think they would love seeing you that way and maybe even have a piece of you"

She moved, indulging him. "That's perfect. There's one other item I want to try."

He reached for the nipple clamps and he finally he got them real tight onto her nipples not too hard that it would hurt her, but tight enough to stay in place. Tight enough so that when he pulled on the chain that joined each clamp to her nipples, that he could pull them off. Something he might try when she was having a full orgasm.

He had another trick up his sleeve that he wanted to try which he had to give credit to his daughter when she was all of five years old. She was playing with her girlfriend, and they played using the flat side of an electric toothbrush. Now, he used the flat part of the toothbrush and placed it on her clitoris in just the right spot. Poppy did a lot of wiggling. He had played with this gadget with other women and knew it was quite stimulating to them. When he finally got her clitoris as hard as he could. He had another trick. it was a cock stimulator and was really meant to go over the man's penis with the vibrator underneath the shaft of the penis. The clap had a space of about eight of an inch in the middle that was flexible to be used as a clamp. He used this gap, to clamp the cock ring onto her clitoris. The cock ring vibrator had four positions of vibrations and it was able to create very strong vibrations even at the low power settings. He started with the lowest.

"How does it feel?

She mumbled something.

As he increased the speed while at the same time, he pulled gently on the chain that was connected to her nipple clamps. He let the vibrator do its job while he slowly increased the speed. You could see by now that she was in exquisite pleasure. He could see by the change in her skin color she was ready to come and at just the right moment he yanked the nipple rings off. She was screaming words but at this time he couldn't hear them. It won't come through the gag. It sounded more like an animal roaring. This was the perfect time. He went down on her and with his tongue slowly, gently, pushed her from one orgasm to another and another until she was quite delirious and then totally spent. It was only then that he took the ball gag out of her mouth and asked her if she was all right.

In a quiet pleading voice. "Can you get these handcuffs off. My wrists are starting to hurt?".

Suddenly, they realized he had a problem. He didn't remember where he put the keys for the handcuffs. She got panicky. He walked away trying to find the keys. When he returned, she was laughing. He noticed that she had gotten out of the hand cuffs.

"How did you do that?"

Still laughing, "I realized all I had to do is squeeze my hand a little bit and I could get them off."

It was another reminder and a lesson that bondage was more in one's head.

Chapter 28

His Turn Or Anal Sex On Him

"Okay you had your fun. Now it's my turn"

What he wanted was to have her fuck him up his ass. He didn't have a lot of experience with that sort of thing, maybe a little. Of course, he experienced something like it, using a butt plug, particularly the larger ones. And some experience with water sports or using his finger up some gal's ass. They seemed to like it ____so how bad could it be. He felt he was ready to have a woman with a strapped-on dildo, give him the treatment.

Of course, being an amateur in this area of anal sex, he thought it be better to start with the smallest dildo. For some reason they had problem getting the dildo to fit into the leather contrivance. The smallest one was the longest dildo that he had available in his collection, and it sort of drooped downwards. It didn't fit well, too small for the gadget. But improvising with additional elastic bands, he got it to work without drooping. He had to consider that she wasn't use to this device. It was a bit weird in design. The real advantage of this model allowed for quick exchanges of different sizes and types of dildos. But one needed a little experience with putting it all together. It had a ring with three straps attached to the ring that held everything in place. The shaft of the dildo went through the center of the metal ring. The large base was held in place by snapping on the straps over the ring in a triangle formation. Then the not too easy part came. That was putting the straps so that they fitted around the body of a woman.

He noticed she was having a little trouble and he was surprised because he thought that she was probably use to doing something like this to other women. He always imagined her as the person, who would be in control. She liked playing the masculine role with women. He just assumed that she would be an expert using a strap on penis with one of her lady friends. After all, she told him about how protective she was with her younger prostitutes. The ones who were learning the business. He really didn't know what she did because she was somewhat secretive about a lot of her intimate sexual experiences. He never was sure what she could do or what she couldn't do. Anyways this was new ground for both of them. She always had high rollers as clients that enjoyed seeing two or more women making love with each other. Many times, it was her job to get things together for the party. She was quite aware that her business was based on repeat customers or word of mouth. So, she knew how to put on a good act. In her youth, like an athlete, she knew she had a limited time to make hay. She was always looking for the next step that would take her to that perfect business. She was good at business. She was no dummy when it came down to making money.

Problems solved and she was ready to go. So, he tried to align himself by her directions to make it easier for her to enter him from behind. She was smart enough to use large amounts of lubricant. She used her fingers to loosen him up. He was surprised how easily and quickly she penetrated him with some minor pain.

Chapter 29

Enema And That Famous General

He had made himself nice and clean back there before anything started. Thanks to his sex shop and he had a gadget that fit on his shower head with a valve that turned it into an enema device. It had a tube that ran into another plastic tube that looked like a slim test tube with multiple holes, about six of an inch in diameter. After many applications of semi hot water, one could be assured that there won't be any embarrassing accidents.

Afterall, as a corpsman, he had to give many enemas while he worked in the hospital. He only had one patient that gave him any problems and that he was a retired four-star general.

He was little surprised how difficult this general was. Giving someone enema wasn't really that easy for him either. He found that most officers of high rank were more than cooperative in taking orders. Most admirals worked with him and later thanked him for doing a good job. Rank for him was not an issue. He tried to treat all patients with respect and do the best he could for them.

It would be much later in his life, before he learned just how important this man was. Of course, at his age and at that time, he had no idea how important he was. But even if he had known, it wouldn't have made any difference. However, he might have used the," Yes Sir", routine more often. It seemed that this man wanted to be respected just because of his rank. Enema was an enema, and his job was to get them as clean as he could. This guy just didn't want to be cooperative.

I guess, if he had to do it today, he would have explained the procedure to the General and why it was so necessary to get his bowels as clean as possible for his procedure. Of course, he was embarrassed, and the General may have thought he was one of those homosexual sailors, but Michael knew that was a kind of Army myth. He himself at that young age was so unaware of anything that was homosexual. Of course, he looked so youthful and clean cut, who knows what this General was thinking. That General had no knowledge of his credentials that he had been accepted into two outstanding medical schools. He learned later in life after studying the history of World War Two. This man always had an ego problem.

Chapter 30

Great Orgasm Or He Got His Moneys Worth

It didn't take her that long; she finally got the knack of it, and she was very gentle, and she seemed to know what she was doing. It was painless. She was good at it. That's why he really loved nurses. They didn't freak out like Wendy, his psychology professor, over body functions. Wendy freaked out every time she went to the bathroom and had to look at her shit. She finally ended up getting a colostomy.

Like him when a nurse saw brown human feces; they understood why it looked so brown. It was a fantastic biological miracle. They knew they were looking at many dead red cells that were produced and died at a phenomenal rate. To be exact, and he remined himself every time he went to the bathroom. One hundred billion (100,000,000,000) are produced in the human body in one hour or nearly 2 billion in a minute. Nurses understood human anatomy.

She was being gentle, and he was feeling the effects of what she was doing to him. To his embarrassment, it was breathtaking, and she seemed to know just how much to push in and to pull out, without every missing a stroke. She did a lot of pulling out, not all the way out, just enough to tease him. It took skill to do that. He knew it was the nurse in her. It wasn't too long before she had gotten the whole dildo inside of him.

Now, she got into it. It wasn't only her strong breathing and her warm breath that he could feel on his back, but he could feel her strength and anger coming through the dildo. As she went deeper inside of him, he heard his own voice, somewhat in a whimpering tone, calling her, a Bitch, over and over. She seemed to like that he was doing that. The more he cried out, he could feel her increasing the tempo.

Why was he calling her, A BITCH, when she was giving him so much pleasure? Shouldn't he be using platitudes like honey, baby, love? She had made him feel vulnerable, and in her control. She had stripped away his ego and he felt disorientated, humble____ where, up was down and down was up. Unconsciously, he resented it or a part of him did. Or was it that he realized something. He was nothing but a speck of dust in the vastness of the universe and the infinity of space and time. Or was it part of the Death Wish that Freud talked about. Or was it being one with his mother, floating in her amniotic fluid. It was embarrassing in sharing all that humility with another person. As a male he should not be feeling those things.

For the first time in his life, he could now understand why women asked to be pounded. She was so strong. Everything she did, felt great. He was amazed how wonderfully exciting it felt. He could feel himself starting to float, losing himself and getting into it. There wasn't much conversation going on. He heard himself making sounds that were disturbing and worse than hearing a recording of his snoring. He said words that he never heard anyone speak. A lot of reference to God and pleading for forgiveness. Having good sex, was one of the few times he felt connected to something else rather than himself. His ego was gone. He was in a kind of a void. Europeans call orgasms, the small death.

Finally, he got to the point where he just became so sensitive to all the pleasure that she was giving him. He didn't want her to stop but he also wanted her to stop. They both seemed to get caught up in the rhythm of things until his pleasure became so intense that he had to have her stop. He was little disappointed with himself because he wanted more but he just couldn't take anymore. He felt like he was going to pass out. That's if he hadn't already done that.

Finally, he heard himself saying, totally out of breath.

"Stop! That's enough! Please stop!"

You could see a puzzled look on her face. She seemed surprised. He was also surprised. She had really gotten into it. He didn't know why he asked her to stop since it felt so good. But somehow his body was saying that it was enough. He couldn't take anymore. He was out of breath. It was comparable to when one has orgasm and then becomes sensitive to the slightest touch. She also reacted that way, after she had a full orgasm. With her, he had learned to have a short break. After having a little time to recover then they could get back into it. They always found the appetite to play some more. They were both capable of having multiple orgasms.

While all of this was going on, he was so happy with himself, that his four hundred dollars, was the best investment that he had ever made. Not only did he discover another layer of Poppy but also another side of who he was. He could never forget that deep pounding that she gave him. There was always a component of anger or aggressiveness when having good sex. Homo Sapiens were aggressive animals. Sex seemed to be a good outlet for all that anger that builds up in the muscles of our body. He always said sex was better than any Xanax.

Chapter 31

The Haunted Light House

It was quite the weekend together. She would later refer to it as one of their best days together. It was something that she wanted to do. It was sort of a mixed bag for him. It was unusual thing; she wanted the experience of being isolated from humanity. Her idea of an adventure was being isolated in a lighthouse in the middle of nowhere.

They were driving up the coast on their way to San Francisco and somewhere near Santa Barbara.

"See that light house out there. They fly you out in a helicopter and leave you there overnight all by yourself."

He knew she had herself admitted to an isolation ward a couple of times because she was fearful of taking her own life. He could see why she might be comfortable being locked up in a cell overnight, but he sure he wouldn't want that experience. So as compromise, they were on their way to East Brother's Lighthouse in the Bay of San Francisco. It was sort of bed and breakfast thing. There would be a manager and his wife and some ten other people who would be isolated on this little island for the whole night.

After they parked the car, there was a little boat waiting and ready to take them to the light house. It was a quaint Victorian building. It was a bit like being in a museum. There were many stories of the past light house keepers' experiences before radar or our modern radio. There were many stories but one that spooked him. The story of when the keeper had to go in for supplies but before he could get back a heavy fog laid in. His wife was stranded without him. The fog was extremely thick that night and its light couldn't cut through the fog. She was all alone and had to manually blow this incredible loud foghorn. The guide blew the horn for them to illustrate just how loud it was. It was scary.

After the lectures and tours, they all had supper together and maybe he drank too much. Poppy retired early and he was too drunk to request sex from her. He didn't sleep well. Whether the place was haunted or not, it didn't matter. He was convinced it was. He had a horrible night between half asleep and sleep but that was not unusual for him. When he slept in a different place, it was always difficult. He kept having nightmares and felt like spirits were coming out of the walls. The one message he got loud and clear from those spirits was he needed to stop his procrastination and sell his Beachwalk Home. After all that nightly badgering from all those different ghosts, he got up early for breakfast while she slept, which was unusual for her. She was always the first to get up. He was still hung over and needed to get some food. He had to make excuses to everyone why Poppy wasn't at breakfast. He decided to be super nice and bring breakfast to her. The group all applauded him for being so gallant. She was surprised and grateful for having something to eat.

After they showered and packed their stuff, they decided to have a final walk around the place. Last night, looking through total darkness, nothing could be, to a greater extent, more scenic than that lite up view of San Francisco and surroundings. The daylight view still was spectacular. She was in a great mood. To his surprise, she had bought her camera and wanted him to take a lot of pictures, her included. That was such a No-No for her.

They were the first to leave. They said goodbye to everyone. They were boated off the island. Michael felt like he was irrevocably on solid ground, far away from that haunted lighthouse and all those ghosts. He let her drive because she was now in one of her moods. It was Big Bear all over again. Not interested in talking, she was giving him the silent treatment that always worked on him. He was getting anxious by the minute. She drove for an hour, and he decided it was time to take a break and have something to drink or eat, so they stopped for lunch

"I don't know what's going on but you're giving me the silent treatment and it's making me anxious and insecure."

"Oh, I didn't know. I just thought you were acting insecure."

After they sat down, as usual she popped one of her, Little Ladies of the Valley, one of those beautiful little heart shaped pills.

"Can I have one too?"

She seemed happy to give him one without much expression. He did what he had learned watching her and placed the Valium underneath his tongue and let it dissolve. She claimed it got into your body quicker.

Fifteen minutes later. "Boy that feels good. I needed that in a big way."

Most of the time when she gave him the silent treatment, he had learned it had something to do with money.

It was a bit embarrassing at the end, when the people who were running the show asked them for a tip.

"You know the only way we survive over here is we need to get tips. Whatever you pay for just pays for our expenses. It only covers the food and what we're charged to rent this place from the association"

From Michael's perspective what he had charged to his credit card was hefty without a tip. He, at that point, expected Poppy to at least offer to pay for the tip but she didn't.

At long last, she was talking to him, and the Valium made them both feel better. He was a little disappointed with her because she didn't add very much to the group. All she told them was her name and her occupation. Her coldness and those ghosts got to him. That was one weekend when he really needed to have his marijuana with him. It wouldn't have been appropriate. It still was illegal. Besides in such confined quarters, the smell of marijuana would have circulated through the air. It was an interesting experience, but he had to put a notch on his belt for something that he would never do again.

Chapter 32

Buying The Engagement Ring

She was fond of getting him little gifts. Poppy, being a collector, found many different opportunities finding unusual knickknacks. Of course, his favorite gifts that he cherished were books that were out of print. When she gave him a gift, it would be wrapped up in beautiful paper exquisitely trimmed with ribbons. It became a ritual for him. The wrapping was always done so exquisitely and for him those wrappings were always a piece of art.

She would remind him from time to time. "You'll find out that I'm very generous."

Poppy seemed to get pissed over his frugality. But he knew that she would find some other suckers that would supply her with the money that she needed. She was like his mother in that she loved to have cash and she also enjoyed counting it. He lived the life using credit cards and never had cash, whereas Poppy paid for everything with hard cash.

By now, he understood this was his disconnection when it came to women. He was comfortable with a woman who understood that he wasn't the kind of man that showered women with gifts. Women expected to be treated well, and to be taken care of. He did not possess that trait and Poppy Always held that against him. Gold and diamonds were overrated possessions to him but not to her. He liked things that were functional, like cars, computers, and other kinds of tools.

So, what happened next was out of character for him. They were in Laguna Hills, and they were in a district where there were loads of jewelry stores. He saw a beautiful engagement ring in the window. He decided that they would go into the shop knowing how Poppy loved to shop. Now that he was inside of the store, he wasn't sure what overcame him. I guess he wanted to impress her and let her know that he wanted to make this into a serious relationship. He asked the jewelry salesman if he could look at a ring.

He pointed. "Yes, it's that ring over there in the window. Could we look at that one please?"

As the clerk pulled the ring out making sure that the center diamond caught enough light so that it sparkled as he presented the ring to Poppy. Michael never saw a ring like that before. It was beautiful. Not only because there was a very large diamond in the center, but because it had all those diamonds that surrounded that big sparkling center diamond.

"This diamond is rated as one of our better ones. There's no flaws in it."

Poppy immediately asked for the clerk's eyepiece. "Can I borrow your magnifying glass?"

She popped the magnifying device to her eye in a very professional way and studied the diamond. He was a bit startled in just how professional she was in handling this small magnifying tube. Something, he never thought of doing. Her professional manner impressed him. She knew what she was doing in the way she handled this jeweler's magnifying scope. Obviously, all of this was nothing new to her. She knew what she was doing, and he was proud of her. But a shiver went down his back, alerting him that something was wrong. He should have listened to this warning. She spent quite a few minutes studying the diamond. She looked up taking the eyepiece out of her eye and smiling.

"Yes, it is a very beautiful diamond. It has a tiny flaw but that's okay."

He asked the clerk. "How much does it cost?"

Six thousand that's inexpensive. We estimate it's worth to be at least twelve. It's on consignment from the owner and he wants six thousand that's including our commission, of course. If you have a friend out of state, we can box it up as if the diamond was there and ship it to your friend. That would save you about six hundred in taxes. Should I reserve this ring while you discuss it with your fiancé?"

She put the ring on her finger and moved her hand around. She acted as if she already owned the ring. She had a rather large smile on her face.

Michael had a ready answer. "Yes, please put it on hold and I'll call you shortly."

When they left the store, he asked Poppy. "What do you think?"

"Oh Michael, it's beautiful! I have never seen anything quite like it."

He always knew money made her happy and she was beaming from one side of her face to the other.

"What I have to do now is see if I can get a loan for six thousand to pay for the ring and then it will be yours."

He had excellent credit, maybe too good. In no time, he had a check for the six thousand. The next Saturday, when she was available, they drove back down to Laguna Beach, and he proceeded to pay for the ring.

The jeweler said, "You know we need to size the ring. We can have that done in about an hour."

He looked at Poppy and then said. "We can go out to have lunch at Las Brisas while they work on it."

The clerk got her exact ring size. Michael noticed she was squirming a little bit at this point. She seemed depressed instead of being happy and she didn't want to leave the ring behind. She seemed to want to leave right away and take the ring with her. He had to coax her to leave.

They decided to walk along the beach and take the scenic route to his favorite restaurant, Las Brisas. It was on the corner of a large cliff looking down and out over the ocean. On a clear day, you could see San Diego. It was a beautiful day, they walked along the beach before they got to the cliff. Once they reached the cliff, a challenge began. They would have to walk up the stone face of this baby to get to the top. And that was exactly where the restaurant rested, on the very top. He noticed that there wasn't any spring in her steps. Poppy was in one of her pensive, thoughtful moods. Poppy didn't say very much at lunch. He had seen that focus look before.

When they were finished eating, they immediately headed to the store. But this time, using the sidewalk, they walked down the hill. At the store Poppy tried on the ring. It was a perfect fit. They then drove to his place. She was really in one of her moods and seemed anxious to get home. He felt disappointed but thought she was just being nervous. He was sure she also wanted to show the ring off to Shirley. It was a big step they were taking. Yet, her response wasn't exactly what he expected. It did seem somewhat strange. But he would soon find out why.

Chapter 33

Poppy Won't Return The Ring

It always happens. When he sees her; there is that spit second, a feeling of mystery that follows her. But today, she looked depressed or maybe she was in deep concentration. Her walk was slow without her usual sleeking, and she was looking more like a boy. He was already seated at the table waiting for her. He had the advantage to be able to look out of the window from inside of the restaurant. He watched her all the way, until she finally sat down next to him. He slid down the booth to make room for her. Their booth was only a few feet from the cash register. It seemed that other people could observe them while people were checking in or checking out. He probably should have selected a more secluded part of the restaurant.

He noticed a couple staring at them. He was particularly sensitive about his own sexuality. He had been called sissy too many times in his life. He grew up at a time when homosexuality was frowned on. He didn't think that he was particularly homophobic; but he came from an environment where people that he worked with or associated with were very anti-homosexual. So, he learned to play both sides of the fence. Most of the time, he was able to be neutral. He had friends who were homosexuals. He felt he was being very tolerant. That was the key word tolerant. Sometimes he felt negativity with some homosexual especially when dealing with more than one of them. He would tell himself that he really didn't care what people did in private.

Poppy was pushing on something in his psychic. He wished that he had been a little more tolerant and especially in his younger years. There could have been some benefit in being bisexual. After all Poppy was bisexual and she skillfully played both sides. But he was beginning to think that Poppy's sexual preference was for females rather than males.

Her comments were. "If you haven't tried it, then don't say anything." And another comment that she made to him. "There's nothing better than sucking on a nice big juicy tit."

He saw her as being the dominant one, but she was such a chameleon that she probably could also be quite submissive. In fact, when they were in the bedroom, she acted very submissively.

He asked, "Someday, can I watch you with a woman?"

"I'm not sure you would like it. Once, I had a boyfriend who did. He broke up with me right afterwards. I guess he didn't like what he saw."

As they were sitting there, one guy was staring at them as he was poking his wife. Now, both the man and the woman started to stare at them. The way they were looking at him gave him the distinct feeling that they were observing a freak. Michael felt as if he was on display, and the couple acted as if they were viewing unusual animals in zoo. Michael realized that Poppy wore no makeup, and her shoes and outfit were very unisexual and drab and rather masculine even for Poppy. He felt very uncomfortable and didn't like being considered being a homosexual. Maybe they were just amazed that they were a couple having a fight over something. Maybe as a couple they were amused seeing another couple fighting in public.

Before this meeting he had a big conversation with two of his renters. Alan was very vehement. "Get that God Dam ring back. If she's not going to marry you then the custom is that she gives the engagement ring back to you."

Before this meeting, he had gone back to the jeweler and asked if he could get some of his money back.

"I can't do that. The ring was on consignment, and I already gave the person his money. My profit was marginal."

Michael didn't really want the ring. Of course, if he had been savvy and understood the jewelry business, he may have made a different discission. But he was emotionally involved and hoping against hope that she would change her mind. Of course, as time went by and into the future, her decision not to marry him would prove to be worth the loss of six thousand dollars. But on that day, at that time, he felt heart broken. Of course, as time went by, he knew that he had been manipulated.

Michael asked her for the ring. She had a tearful look on her face. The ring was sized so perfectively that she had difficulty getting it off. She finally handed it to him. He should have just pocketed it the ring, but he hesitated. Seeing the sad look on her face, he thought maybe there was a chance that they could work out their differences. He thought that she was just not ready. That maybe in time she would change her mind. Maybe, they could work out their differences. He felt sad too. He wasn't ready to break with the dream, the illusion. He would pay the price for that moment of hesitation.

Later he would accept what she told him.

'You're not really interested in marrying me. You were only interested in keeping your house at Beachwalk."

There was a lot of Truth to that. He remembered after the kids grew up particularly after his son moved out; he had to get renters to keep the payment up. His son was nice enough to give him rent money. He felt that he was married to the bank, and that the bank really owned the house. He couldn't even afford to pay the taxes on the house, and he didn't pay the taxes. He kept putting off the property tax from year to year but by doing that he was accumulating quite a sum of money in interest by not paying it off. The whole ridiculous thing was that at the beginning his payments were super low around $650 a month. He kept refinancing the house in order to pay off his credit cards because of his dating and living beyond his means.

It would take time, accompanied with a lot of pain, but in the end, he would agree that she was right on. He would finally accept the idea that the pain of moving and losing his Beachwalk Home was far greater than the pain of losing her.

She managed to keep the ring. Later, she even came up with a story that she passed out at a party, and someone stole the ring. He could have gone to his insurance company and make a claim. But his move in avoiding paying taxes by sending the receipt to his buddy in Washington; didn't give him that option. He thought her story about the thief was a lie. She never reported the ring stolen and besides what could he have done about it. She saw an opportunity to get something from him. It was part of her nature. She saw an opportunity and took it. He was playing with fire, and he had to accept it. He kept thinking of their good trips together. But somewhere and someday in reality, he would have to accept that he had been taken for six thousand dollars. And at this moment, he surely wasn't thinking that he got away cheap; nor, was he thinking that he would have his Beachwalk Home if he married her, but a monster would be living inside of it. She would turn into a Wendy. You didn't see the monster, only just a flash, like a strobe. You would eventually see this serpent with fangs squirting poison at you or the big teeth of a shark or the Medusa and instead of hair on her head there were all those snakes hissing at you.

He remembered that she told Shirley.

"I found the person that I want to marry."

He was sure she meant it at the time. But that mood was short lived learning the hard way just how fickle she was. And he should have known better. He would never be able to make enough money to satisfy her. He was already maxed out on his credit cards. Property taxes were due on his house, and he would have difficulty paying that bill. He had backed himself into a hole. He remembers Wendy talking about Rick who she finally married and how he found himself broke after dating so many different WOMEN. Dating is expensive something that no female is welling to acknowledge. The lies that our society makes us believe that the man must be the financial giver. In the end the price that the man must pay for lying to himself and to women when he thinks he is in love. There is a price for everything

Pat Allan, PSYCHOLOGIST, a famous Orange County speaker preached.

"Women take and men give. At least when it comes down to money."

Or

"Beauty gets money and money gets beauty."

Chapter 34

Fortune Teller And Listening To The Tape

Michael met Poppy at her home, and he was anxious to know what Maria said. She was that fortune teller that Poppy put so much faith in with her predictions

"She told me a lot of interesting things. Some of the things I already knew."

She presented Michael with the tape from her last session.

"Here it is."

She had a strange look on her face. "Why don't you listen to it while you drive down to Laguna. Shirley decided that she wanted to go to the reading. Since you would have to drive back here, it makes more sense if you drive by yourself. Shirley and I will drive together. In that way you will be closer to Huntington Beach."

He felt a bit weird about Shirley going to the READING. He would miss Poppy's company, but it didn't make any sense to have Shirley drive by herself. He didn't quite understand the weird relationship she had with Shirley; it always seemed strange. At the last READING, Shirley came by herself. She never asked to join them. Okay, so this time he would be the third man out. He didn't like it, but there wasn't anything he could do about it

Still, he tried to put a good face on it. He would be able to listen to the tape and he was excited to find out about their future together; so, he thought. But he also had premonition that this was not a good sign. Poppy was acting in that weird mood, like she didn't want him there at the READING. It wasn't that unusual for her; she had her moods. Part of him didn't care. She was sort of an experiment. He really wanted to understand her. He didn't want to get in her way. It was like talking to a known criminal and trying to understand what motivated him. He continued to feel sorry for her and tried not to be sucked into her sickness. He knew he was getting out of control. He understood that he needed to monitor what he was doing. Fortunately, he just didn't have that deep infatuation for her. Even though he tried to free himself from any though of a life with her; he felt like he was being dragged in as if he was being caught in an undertow, and no matter, how much he tried he couldn't get free. He didn't want to live her life. He should have never met her family, that was a lot of cold water. And as much as he tried to imagine life with her, he wasn't comfortable in what he saw. He should have never gotten her the ring.

His intuition was correct. He became disturbed listening to the tape.

Maria: "My, there is no moss growing under your feet. I see many men. I see one." She laughed.

"I see another one. He seems very exciting and adventuresome. I can see why you are excited by him. It seems that he has just lately come into a small fortune. Something sporty about him. Oh yes, I see you and him on a motorcycle."

He heard a light giggle from Poppy.

All he heard was that there were many men in her life and more to come. There was no forecast of a future for them. He was beside himself and was becoming furious with Poppy. By now, he had learned just how fickle she really was. But up to the present time, he had assumed that she had put him in a special position. Now he was confronted with the knowledge that she was inundated with men, and he felt that he was on his way out.

Why did she let him listen to this? But they he shared other tapes like this. They had been honest with one another. And like her, he was a believer in fortune telling. It's easy to see your future. We are fantastic computers. All one needs to do is add in our history, our genes, our childhood, our conditioning, our dreams. Walla, there is your future, give and take a bit.

She had always been wishy washy over her commitment to him.

"Michael why don't we just hang out together. I'm sure something good will come from it."

At first, he thought why not. He had nothing better to do. He really thought from the beginning that the relationship wouldn't go anywhere. He saw that right from the beginning that they were totally different.

But as he got to know her, she seemed to disarm him. Later he was used to seeing that knowing look on her face. The look, that told him that she had power over him. He was really one of her helpless victims. He could never understand where she got that kind of power. But he felt that he was falling in love with her. She had a boyish temperament and that was very disarming. She seemed to sense what men wanted and when it pleased her, she was very willing to oblige them.

Chapter 35

On Their Way To Newport And The Poem Reading

They were now on the Freeway, with Shirly driving her new Mercedes. She was in the car in front of him. He was right behind them as they were entering the Santa Ana Freeway. Freeways always made him feel queasy, betting on his survivability, going sometimes over ninety miles an hour. It was always plain, SCARY.

They were heading south for Laguna Beach. It was always difficult to figure where the correct turn off was for the Beach without turning on his GPS but since Shirley was driving; he decided all he needed to do was to follow her.

He could see that they were having a very animated conversation. He always suspected that Shirley and Poppy were intimate in a sexual way or had been.

He was told by some cheap fortune teller that are always available at charity events. He had described his feelings to this interesting middle-aged reader.

How could anyone tell the future. The only way he could explain that was that it worked out to be a good guess, or they were tuning into something. He did believe in ESP and someway they were able to tap into that. It's also possible the future already happened, and we can only see time in our continuous serial linear pattern instead of looping or whatever it does.

The Psychic continued. "Yes, they do have a very close relationship. It's more like mother and child relationship. It's too bad because they are good for each other, but unfortunately, I sense the ending to that relationship.

(Author's note: Strangely, in the future when Poppy gave her notice to Shirley and moved out. A couple months later, Shirley died of pancreatic cancer.)

"It's common for women to share an intense closeness without having sex together. I don't see anything sexual in their relationship. It's more like a mother daughter relationship."

He didn't mention that Shirley was a much older woman.

"It's too bad, I do see a brake in their relationship. Someone is going to be really hurt; I feel sorry for both of them."

They were still whizzing along on this freeway and so was his temper and his thoughts. By the time, they had reached their destination he didn't want any part of them and to his amazement neither did they. Poppy simply ignored him. He could feel how she had fallen under Shirley's control. Probably it was better that he should be there by himself, using separate cars.

He finally parked his car and made sure he put enough money into the meter. He had saved a bunch of quarters for this very moment. With quarters jiggling in his hand, he had learned to fill a meter up with quarters. He knew that most beach communities made a sport of collecting big fines on meters that went into the red zone. The meters had big red flag, a visible signal for the ubiquitous meter maids,

They finally entered together, and it was on the second floor. The room was dark. Even though, the room was large the acoustics were excellent. It was a micro-brewery, and they had all the free popcorn that you could eat. Boy, he loved that popcorn. The room was packed with over fifty people. He noticed a pair of attractive young women. He could tell by their attitude and overhearing their introduction that they were celebrity readers from Chicago. They were on a tour.

Shirley settled in the back of the room, and he joined them. Poppy looked straight ahead somewhat ignoring him. He decided to go out for drinks. He proceeded to the bar. When he came back, Shirley was unusually friendly toward him trying to neutralize Poppy's coolness.

Chapter 36

The Full Moon

All readings were excellent and in the atmosphere of such wonderful artist. He knew the pattern; Poppy would never get up to read. In fact, both Shirley and he were on the same side. They both wanted to see Poppy recognized for her abilities. But he knew and Shirley knew that from past experiences, for whatever reason, she would not get up to read her stuff. Poppy like most people talk the good story but would do little to follow it up with real action.

At one meeting he got so disgusted with her that he got up and read two of her poems. He received great applause from the audience because her writings were not only good but superior to everything else that was presented. So, he decided to repeat himself and read one of her poems.

He got up to the microphone and explained to the audience that his son was getting married the following weekend and he decided to compose a poem with Poppy's help, a poem for his son's wedding.

When the Moon is Full

There comes a Time

And A Place

To Feel Full

To Have Enough

To Be Yourself

Not To Only Wish

But To Also Do

What is RIGHT

Not Only For You

But

For All

For

Those Before

And

For Those After

Love

Real Love

It's A Wonderful Thing

So don't be fooled

It gives You Strength

To Do

What's Right

Not only for yourself

But For All

So now

With the Moon so Full

So Bright

So, Round

Oh

Just So Full

There can only be

One Universe

And

Only the Full Truth

The exquisite Harmony

The Balance

Please

No More Lies

In the Light

Of the Full Moon

Why should there be

Anything but

What's right

What's true

What fits

I know

Some of you

Will never see

It's for us

Who can see

To tell the Truth

We may not be able

 to change

What's now

But our Thoughts will

So will our deeds

They will slowly

Permeate into Life

Like a beautiful fragrance

Digging deep into everything

We will have our SAY

You

And You

May never smell it

But like a Van Goth Painting

Their colors and their brilliance

Over the Years

Will slowly

penetrate

into every molecule

Over and over

This Abundant Universe

Because

The Truth

It never LIES

It Is why will always FIT

So, Fear not

If you are not ready

For like a fragrance

It will linger in your mind

Until One Day

 Someday

Maybe even today

You will Sense

The Balance

that's There

It's never too Late

Thoughts are Eternal

 Not ephemeral

and You To

Will See

the truth

and

Someday

You too

Will be freed

When he was done, he received a tremendous applause. He was very pleased with himself. He looked over at Poppy and she had her non-plus facemask on; however, Shirley beamed with a big smile showing appreciation for his talent. He moved towards Poppy, but she seemed cold and reserved. This was not that usual because she was never demonstrative in public

The group was closing, and Shirley and Poppy started to exit. He said goodnight in a very strained way. They just continued to ease out and away. He felt that she preferred to be with Shirley.

They left and moved quickly and finally they were a block ahead of him. He continued his walk, in deep thought. Not realizing it; he had overtaken them, and he caught them browsing looking at one of the displays in the store's window. They smiled at him as he passed by. He tried not to ignore them, but he felt that he was in one of his pouting moods. They gave him a knowing look. Looking back at this moment, he would always feel the hurt and betrayal.

Poppy probably gave him the tape because she was honest about their relationship. She was unsure of her feelings. He had known from the beginning that she had difficulty in making any real commitments.

It was always a sad thing. When she was with him. He felt that no one could be closer to him. She seemed to be content and happy. Sometimes, it would take only a few hours before it wore off. At rare moments, her love might last a week but from his experience never lasted longer than that.

Chapter 37

Frank, Poppy's New Friend

Poppy knocked on his door. Frank was excited to see her. It had been a while since he had wanted to date someone. She seemed so friendly and easy going. He could tell that she was adventuresome. When they first met, she hopped on the back of his bike as if she had ridden one every day.

He could tell right away in the way she acted that she was bisexual. He liked that. His ex-wife, Patricia was that way. Patricia was so beautiful that he would do almost anything for her, and he enjoyed playing that game with her. His wife and he would go out on the prowl together. Looking for someone that would fit. It was easy to do that since she had impeccable taste and with her looks and body, she was able to get almost any woman or couple she wanted.

He was in a very good position. He didn't have to work. He and his father ran their business well together. Rental properties were easy to run. At least, he found that to be his forte. He was a regular at the council meetings at Newport Beach. Everyone knew him well and they also took special care of him. He never had any problems in Newport Beach. He knew quite a few of the policeman.

He missed Patricia. Well, he could understand. After that surfing accident. She was not this type of person to stick around and live with a cripple. In any case he missed her, and Poppy reminded him of her. Of course, Patricia would eventually want to come back. After all, he had enough money to take care of her but towards the end of their relationship she was doing massive quantities of drugs. Most of the time he didn't even know who she was.

Chapter 38

Back From Her Date

After listening to that tape and their visit to Laguna everything started to unravel quickly. All he heard on that tape was all the different men she had going for her. She seemed to be very much infatuated with the guy on the motorcycle. She was spending an overnight with him. Poppy was honest about what was happening in her life particularly with her different affaires. They both had that sort of honesty together that they were able to be friends and not fearful of the other relationships.

"I know what I was doing. I can't say that by going over there I didn't know what I was doing. I'm a big girl now."

He was trying to imagine what went on, but he knew if he was patient, he would hear the full story.

"Can you imagine he told me he wanted me to have his baby?"

The way she said it, Michael realized that she might be considering the possibility. Of course, that was her chameleon side talking. In a couple of days, the story would be different.

"Frank told me about his ex-wife. She was a model and bisexual. They would go to bars together and try to find someone. He told me how she liked sharing her friends with him."

"What happened to her?"

"He had surfing accident and part of his brain was damaged. She left him while he was recovering. At first, he couldn't talk. He talks fine now but he has little bit of a lisp. He goes surfing every day. He never misses a day. He and his father own a whole block of buildings there in Newport Beach right near the pier. He is a member of the Newport Council. He is funny. He has an unusual sense of humor. He told me something last night. It was something I needed to hear. It built up my confidence. He likes to put stickers everywhere."

She started to giggle as she looked inside of her shoe. "It's still there." She laughed some more.

She was serious now as she looked at Michael. "I know I asked myself why I'm looking when I have everything, I wanted right in front of me. "

At this point he was so confused that he wasn't sure of who she was talking about but guessed it might be about him. He guessed this was her way of asking him for forgiveness. It was her way of offering him an apology. But everything with Poppy had a short half-life.

A few more days went by. He was at Poppy's place when her phone went off. For some reason she wanted him to hear the conversation between her and Frank. He had sort of a stutter. From the tone of his voice, he sounded rather angry.

"Look" he said, "When you get sober then let's talk. I just can't stand it when you're slurring your words because you're drunk."

He hung up she looked at him in disbelief." Do I sound drunk?"

"No"

That was just weird. All Michael could think of is this guy must be very straight and not into drugs. Well, that probably was the end of her Motorcycle Dude.

Chapter 39

Being Jealous

Later, time went on. Michael's relationship with Poppy was getting tricky. It was another one of their confrontational conversations. They just finished with their talk. After he hung up, he was disgusted with himself. He brought up the fact that Joe was a police officer and Michael thought that he was better than that. He had to ask himself again. Why was he doing this thing with Poppy? What was going on? Now, he was acting jealous, and he didn't know why he was doing that. OK, he had become addicted to her. In the same way that he ended up smoking three packs of cigarettes a day. He finally kicked the habit, but he was troubled by nightmares. One day, the nightmares just stopped. It took fifteen years before they stopped. Yet for fifteen years, in his dream, he would be at a bar; someone would offer him a smoke. He would take the cigarette and light up. Of course, that dream would wake him up in the middle of the night.

It always struck him how strange it was when you are addicted to something. While you were under the spell of the addiction, you never could see the negative parts of your addiction. It was only later that the negatives became obvious. With cigarettes, it was the holes in his garments from the hot ashes from the cigarettes. Then, there was the filth in the ash trays and hideous smell from smoking.

The need to take so many breaks for smoking. Or the amount of money smoking cost. He was wondering what insights he would have ten years from now about their relationship. He hoped by then she would be out of his system.

He was trying to make a case that he was better than Joe because he wasn't a policeman. He was ashamed in that he was stereotyping policemen as sort of downtrodden.

He asked Wendy, as a professor of communications at Long Beach State University, what is your experience with policemen. "When they come to my classes, they are very dedicated to helping people. Of course, that's before they get harden."

Michael had to come to his senses and understand that they saw the worst in people, drunk, drugged up, stealing and even the killing of other people. The fact that human beings had to have policemen to keep law and order was just another indicator of how nuts we are. It showed the flaws of being a human. We need to have a policeman to regulate us to make sure that bad things didn't happen. When bad things happen, they had to be there and sometimes they killed people in order to protect other people. On top of that the cities didn't want to spend the money that was necessary to pay the policemen. The cities were always trying to save money. So, they never paid enough money for training. That was Michael's hot button, he had worked for a training company, and he found most companies didn't budget enough money for training. He knew few police departments wanted to spend money for proficient training. Which would include simulation not just a written test, training that included simulations and used play acting techniques. Police got a bad rap because they weren't trained properly. Yet, the cities would end up paying millions of dollars in court never learning the true cost from sloppy training.

There was also a lot of peer pressure to be macho. They piled on a lot of duties that police should never be involved with. The cities encouraged them to write all kinds of tickets. Every time there was a recession, cities came up with all kinds of creative ways to increase revenue. They used the police to give out tickets just so they could get extra money and he would see the police giving out a lot of tickets for speeding, choosing spots were they knew they could catch people. There were many pressures on the police. And then people wondered why there were so many unnecessary killings. They were overworked and abused by the system in order to save money. Cities were always cutting corners, when things got tight of course they laid off the policeman and made it more difficult for the few that were still on duty.

Michael knew he could never be a police officer. He just didn't want that kind of responsibility but unfortunately someone had to do it. He had to get off his high horse. He had to give Joe credit for what he did. He had to face it.

He had to consider what Poppy admitted. "I wish I could have both of you in one person."

He had to be honest. Knowing Poppy, Joe was far the better choice for her. It was hard for Michael to swallow that bitter pill. With Joe she would be able to give up her nursing job.

Chapter 40

Poppy's Hypochondrical Behavior And Her Mother

Poppy insisted that she had ovarian cancer and that she had to have her uterus removed. Michael went with her on her different consultation. Of course, any kind of surgery is serious but for Poppy this operation seemed to be life or death. Since he was so involved with her medically, he assumed that he would visit her in the hospital.

He didn't quite remember how it happened, but it was obvious that he wasn't going to be there. It was going to be Joe's honor. It was obvious that her mother, Ann did not wish him to be there. He could understand; she did not see him as a potential provider.

He decided to call and speak with Poppy's mother. After some small talk, her reply was.

"I don't even know who you are."

At This point in desperation, he told her "I bought Poppy a rather expensive engagement ring, so I don't quite understand why you don't know who I am."

She then got very huffy and said. "What does that have to do with me? Why are you calling me?"

The conversation was getting very hot. Her husband got on the phone and in a very sober and soothing voice.

"I know that something was going on between you and Poppy. Someone wouldn't spend as much money as you did for that hotel room that you guys had in Ventura. I think the best bet is to wait while all of this going on, until after the operation. Maybe then, we can get together and have supper and discuss the whole matter."

He knew at this point; he was acting stupidly. Despite the pain he was in, he had to get a hold of himself. When he first met Poppy, she told him what she wanted and that was just to hang out together and that's worked well. He now knew he had crossed the line. That's why in the beginning, it had worked for so long. Back then he really didn't care that much about her and that's what made the relationship so magical.

Chapter 41

Poppy Is Pissed Off

They were on their second pitcher of beer. He liked the fact that she tried to keep up with him. She was a fraction of what he weighed, and today the alcohol seemed to have little effect on her. He seemed to be attracted to those strong tough (drink you under the table) type of woman. He guessed that's how he saw his grandmother when he was a little boy. She would guzzle down several glasses of beer. Then without missing a beat, she would continue the chores at hand. He admired Poppy's toughness in that same way. He was comfortable with the fact, that she could take care of herself. He knew that was selfish of him. He also knew that was why strong women were attracted to him; whereas most women wanted to feel that their man was strong and could protect them. Of course, Poppy enjoyed the reverse role and wanted to be in charge some of the time. And today was the day, she wanted to be the boss.

She squealed. "You wanted my mother to kiss your ass!"

"Yah, I did. I think that I'm a lot better than that cop friend of yours."

"You don't understand Joe! He goes way back. They have a relationship with him. They felt he could take care of me, and they thought I was going to marry him. And they still do. It was part of their program. I think it was wonderful the way they came out to meet you when they knew I was still dating Joe. You don't give them credit for what they did and who they are."

"Now you're going into the hospital and Joe is going to drive you! He's going to be there?"

"If that is going to bother you so much than I'll get Mary or Shirley to drive me."

"But you don't want me there?"

"No, I don't because I know what an asshole you will make of yourself in front of my mother and my step-father. I'll have my sister call you or text you to let you know that everything is alright."

Then, with a deep breath. "I wish you could have some of Joe's good qualities mixed in with your good qualities, that person would be just perfect!"

He knew what she was referring to. Joe was very generous with his money, and he wasn't. That remark really got to him. It was real.

She started to raise her voice again and in anger, she lifted a dish and bounced it off the table and it made a thud but didn't break

His eyes widen but he felt one person making a scene was enough. He heard the workers giggle behind the wall. And he heard a guy say. "Boy, she really giving him shit."

He saw that she also heard their comments and that fed her power over him. It gave her a gleefulness to have her advantage.

He just knew that something didn't sit right. She had told him that she had broken off with Joe twice and yet somehow Joe was still in the picture. He really didn't mind her relationship with Joe, but he did mind her dishonesty. Now, that she was going into the hospital for the removal of her ovaries and uterus with a good possibility that she had cancer. Now his relationship with her was strained.

Last year, she had muscular dystrophy. She couldn't feel a part of her body. Then she was going to become a cripple and now she was going to die from cancer.

Or her, "I am going to commit suicide."

This new crisis with the cancer and her hysteria about dying. It went on and on. Inwardly, unconsciously, he wanted Joe to have her or even someone else. With all her psychological problems and now this cancer bit, it was too much for him.

She had a hold on him, something concerning his addictive personality. It could have been the sex. Unfortunately, it was more than that. She had managed to get into his head, and she was playing with him. He didn't know if all men were weak in this way, and she was just clever and took advantage of their venerability. She had managed to have a profitable career as a prostitute. She knew how to keep a man's attention. Wasn't that all part of her trade?

Yes, she had appealed to his dark side. She had found those little secrets in him that he didn't even know existed. Some friends called her a witch and she even claimed to be a female devil. She was a handful and he kept asking himself what was in it for him. He knew he had to break away. Yes, there was a part of her that he liked. BUT his psychologist warned him that if he managed to fix her then he would become bored with her. He was in fact a person that needed his interest peeked. He would eventually find her boring. He felt confused because at one point he felt that she loved him. In turn, she was bringing out feelings in him that he had not felt before. His psychologist warned him that she was unavailable. That in fact he was attracted to unavailable women. Poppy constantly had warned him that she was unavailable for love.

"How can I love you when don't even love myself?"

Ruth, his psychologist warned him. "You are like a moth attracted to a flame. It is your nature. You need to make it clear to women that you are dating. You are not open to a loving relationship, but that you can have friends. I'm a firm believer that we can modify our behavior, but you need more time with yourself and to find yourself."

Chapter 42

The Safe And Poppy Counting Her Money

Or

The Lost Engagement Ring

They arrived home exhausted from their little combat at the Pizza place. She liked sex and he did too. He watched her in her excitement. He could feel that she enjoyed doing something that shouldn't be done. Afterall, Shirley was home, and he knew it was against the rule of having visitors.

The ritual began, the candles were lit and then she chose the right music for the occasion. The blankets were pulled back. A towel was placed in the middle of the bed. He started to undress, as she prepared herself. Placing his clothes in a neat pile for his getaway when everything was finished. She would make him leave as soon as they were done. It was one of the rules of the house, no overnight guest. That worked for him; because, he had to get up early the next morning. He was a one-hour drive from his home in Huntington Beach. It would be two o'clock in the morning by the time he went to bed.

He had to be quiet because he knew Shirley could hear them if they were not super quiet. He always had to keep it in the back of his head that Shirley and Poppy were involved in something. Poppy was extremely quiet when she was in her own bedroom.

She had her legs prominently spread out, with her pussy staring at him. There were times when she was very aroused. He could tell when that was because when he touched her there, she was like a man, and she would be wet with secretions. He could never figure exactly what brought on this special arousal. She felt venerable to him. He could arouse her with his touch or his voice. Maybe her performance was brought on by drugs? He knew she was always on something from painkillers to Valium. He had no comprehension of what heroin would do but he knew now that she shot heroin mixed in with coke.

She had a talent of responding openly to her tiniest passion. If he had to pinpoint his addiction to her, it was the way she read him. She would amorously respond to everything he would do. It was so rewarding for him to hear her deep moans and then her squirming. He felt like he was pleasuring her and at that moment she could not resist him. And of course, there was his illusion that she would be his forever. He knew this was not the case but at that moment, that's what he felt. He felt that he was part of her and she in turn was part of him.

OOPS, a reminder would go off in his head. It was Ruth's voice, his psychologist. "You must remember that she is a chameleon. When she feels those things with you, she really does. But she has no core. There isn't anyone there. She becomes a reflection of you.

When you leave, you're gone. You are no longer there. I feel sorry for her. Can you imagine how lonely she is?"

After having her orgasm, as always, the mood shifted to business (no kisses, no platitudes). She put on her robe, and he put on his clothes, and he was ready to leave.

She stopped him. "I want to show you something."

She went to her closet and in the corner, hidden behind her clothes; he saw a major duty safe. He saw that it had a large combination dial plus a key lock. It was made of thick steel and stood about four feet in height and two feet in width.

She explained, "It's bolted to the floor. No one is going to move that safe."

She went through quite a ritual just getting it open. He though he heard the clicks as she rolled the dial feeling for the right combination. He thought that it was unusual for someone to have such a large safe, especially in a rented room, until he saw what was in it. He heard the final click as she pulled the door open.

"My mother always said I had a good taste for things when I was five. She said I was always mesmerized by a large chandelier when we went shopping."

She threw out bundles of wrapped one-hundred-dollar bills, Benjamin Franklins. He was looking at a mountain of money. At least, five hundred thousand dollars, if not more. It was more cash than he had ever seen in his whole life. So much money, the most money he ever carried was forty dollars. He used credit cards for most of his transactions.

He was feeling sick. He didn't like money and even worse he didn't like counting it. Poppy counting that money brought back memories of when he was four years old. The memories of his mother counting money. Especially, that day when his mother counted his father's weekly earnings.

Just before his father came home from work. His aunt, his mother's sister, seemed to be drilling her.

"You know what to say? When he comes home, simply ask him to show his earning for the week."

It was Friday and he knew it was pay day. He wasn't sure why his aunt was there and sort of drilling his mother that way. He was alone with his mother when his father came home. His father laid his earnings on the table, and she seemed to be counting what was there on the table. That's when his mother confronted his father about his drinking. She already heard through the grapevine that he was fired from his job because of his drinking. She seemed calm and determined to say what his aunt instructed her to say. After the talking was over, she threw all his clothes down the stairs. Then, told his father to leave.

He remembers his father pleading with her. "Can't I even have that picture of Junior?" It was large, framed photograph that was on display in the kitchen.

"No, you don't deserve having a son."

When he finally got outside, in her anger she ran to the porch and threw the remainder of everything he owned on the outside lawn. He remembers her crying and felt all that confusion inside of him. Just recently his pet dog was killed, hit by a car and his grandfather passed on from cancer, and now his father was also gone. He felt that was a lot for a four-year-old to understand.

He was watching Poppy while she swooped up two hundred thousand and put it into an envelope. "This is for my mother."

She picked another sixty thousand and placed into another envelope. "This is for my sister."

She stuffed another envelope.

"Twenty thousand for my brother that he was asking for. I would give him more, but he pissed me off the other day when he said I could afford to loan him money since I was a prostitute and I could afford it, since it wasn't really my money."

She pulled out a cloth pouch and then pulled out a Smith Wesson. It had a polished silver appearance and to him resembled a canon. "My husband and I bought this. It shoots magnums and that will go through steel. It will stop anyone with one shot. I'm going to give this to Joe. I know how he appreciates guns."

"And for you." And she paused filled with sarcasm. "I know how you love jewelry." He hated jewelry.

She pulled out the box that he had remembered. It was his engagement ring. She put the ring on her finger. He had forgotten how beautiful it looked.

She teased him with. "It is sized so perfectly that it's almost impossible to take off."

Seeing the ring, he thought, well at least she hadn't sold it. At that very moment, he foolishly thought that she cared for him. If she ever called him on it, he probably would still marry her. He wished he could look deep inside of himself to understand to see just how committed he was to her. He knew that she also knew that if she wanted, she could have him marry her.

He never asked to have the ring back. WHY?

Because, by now, he knew that was her price for making love with him. Courtesans have lived that way for years. Like Geishas, they were very high-end fun girls. He was the one that chose to play with fire and that was the price of the ticket. It would be many years later that he would understand that he was lucky. If the relationship had gone further, how much more would that have cost him?

"Well, Michael here's all my jewelry."

He was momentarily nauseous, once more. It all looked like junk except for his ring. There wasn't a pretty piece among them, not one colorful stone. Nothing but some small diamonds and gold bracelets, watches, and necklaces. And there were boxes and boxes of pearls in all forms, necklaces, earrings, bracelets, and everything in between. He never thought that pearls were that expensive and he knew they could be worn with almost any kind of clothing and all kinds of occasions, but why did she collect so many of them.

Ruth said. "Prostitute are addicted to money. It's getting money for sex that drives them. They aren't interested in anything else."

He felt stupid. He was smart enough to know the value of money and what it could get you, but he'd like thinking that he was above it all. Poppy always liked putting his nose into it, making him feel like he was cheap. Of course, he knew that the relationship was ending but it was like using a frayed rope. You could use it over and over but each time it became a little weaker until it finally just broke.

He had one relationship where the woman said. "I decided that rather than let this relationship take it's natural course my intuition tells me to end it now."

It was the cold turkey approach, and he should have done that tonight. Just say goodbye and move on. But he could not. He knew it was a weakness on his part. He always went for the long shot. He was a dreamer.

As he was leaving, she gave him a piece of paper. It was another one of her poems.

"I like you to have this. "

Attraction

When we first met, I thought_____ you must be kidding, haven't we met somewhere before?

We had spoken several times before "getting together" so once we did, a lot had already been said.

I don't know what I was looking for

Still don't

Maybe that really doesn't matter because what does?

We seem to possess.

The Dance of Intimacy, The Dance of Anger

(both books I've never read).

Hopscotch and The Tug of War. Oh, how I love to stretch beyond my limits. (Whatever those are?)

You make me real.

You make me fake.

Making me feel like I can really pull it off_____ at any time.

And I do!

You notice because I do it, to you too!

I see the little boy.

Trying to be *a Man.*

I'm your mother, your baby-sitter, your Lover tuned into all your fantasies.

I am also your Hopes, Dreams, your Last Chance _ and best of all. I am your worst nightmare (in living color).

Yet____ most importantly I'm your best friend all rolled up into one.

How could we possibly deny this "attraction"!

Why would we even want too?

Poppy

Chapter 43

Hotel Coronado And Christmas

He had learned after many relationships that when things seemed to be going well, one brushed the negatives underneath the rug. They were going to Coronado for Christmas. On their way, they were going to stop at Laguna for a poetry session sponsored by one of his professors from his English class. This professor also owned a bookstore and formed a group that did book reviews. They had meetings once a month and it was critiques, on different Spanish Latin American authors. The group was made up of women from all different countries of Latin America, Cuba, Argentina, Puerto Rico, and Mexico. Ramon was a firm believer that California and Texas belonged to Mexico and someday that real-estate would become a state within the state. Michael found it fascinating that the women of the group were of Spanish heritage, but they had a different viewpoint on the male-female relationships within the family.

When they had a break and Poppy went to the rest room, Ramon told him just how fascinated he was with Poppy. He just couldn't say enough wonderful things about her and how lucky Michael was in knowing someone like Poppy

That made Michael feel odd since he had just had a big fight with Poppy while driving there.

"You know we're not having as much fun as we used to. I think that you're avoiding me a lot and even when you're with me, you're not with me."

Poppy didn't say anything.

When they finally got to the venue and parked the car. Poppy grabbed him and then brushed up against him, in a deep hug, and cuddled him. There was something about the way she did that. It just made him feel very warm all over and he was alright.

After the reading they proceeded to Coronado, a trip that again was going to cost him a bundle of hard-earned money, but it was a fantastic hotel with a wonderful, from floor to ceiling, decorated Christmas Tree in the main lobby.

He had an old girlfriend Donna that he knew from the time she was thirty years old. She now was in her late forties still very attractive good looking and well-educated and had a great physique. He wanted to show Poppy off to her. Donna brought along a boyfriend. She always had a boyfriend to pick up the tab. She was a little bit like Poppy except that she was very monogamous. She always went for money or fame.

After they settled in. Donna said to Poppy in his presence, in not a joking manner. "You must have something going for old Cheapo to take care of you, this way."

Poppy was enchanted with Donna. "Boy, I would like to get down on her."

Of course, He told Donna what Poppy told him. He knew that wasn't a big deal. Donna was often hit on by other women.

"Oh, that ugly thing. I think not."

He never repeated Donna's comment. He just let Poppy dream on as she explained what she sexually wanted to do with Donna.

It turned out to be a wonderful evening even in bed. Unfortunately, sometime later with a bit of anger; Poppy reminded him of that night

"I was wonderfully in love with you and the sex was beautiful until you asked me to stick my finger up your ass. I couldn't believe it, here I had a great orgasm and felt madly in love with you, and you did that to me."

He said nothing in his defense. He thought of his insensitivity, but he also realized how strange the relationship had become.

As she was talking, he was thinking of how all relationships have cracks, like concrete. He was told by contractors that cement was really composed of many tiny cracks and most cracks were invisible and those that became visible were because of stress.

CHAPTER 44

Poppy And The Oscars

The night of the Academy Awards. A limousine drove up, the door opened, and Poppy rushed into the limousine. She didn't want anyone in the neighborhood and particularly Shirley, to notice this big black limousine.

As she popped in, she was greeted. "Hey gal, it's been a long time since Vegas. I told you that I could get you to the Oscars. Sorry it took so long, this is Barbara, Sandra and this is Poppy. Poppy gave us a lot of good times at the parties she arranged when I was in Vegas. I will never forget that night you got all my friends a date and they were all gorgeous women. I got something special for you. We all shared some of it already; it's good stuff. Right girls?"

Barbara and Sandra just giggled. "We already had a head start before you." He passed on a snuff bottle. "Take as much as you want it's a long drive to LA and we all want to have a little fun together. Who do you like Barbara or Sandra? They are both beautiful. I sort of know your taste. I think you'll like Sandra. You two will make a great couple."

CHAPTER 45

Another Victim

Poppy And The Widower

"Boy, did I hit a gold mine. I met this man whose wife just recently passed on. He manages a store that people call when a close relative passes on. He gets to go in and pick up all of the items from the family. They just want someone to take the stuff. Sometimes it's just junk, but occasionally there are some good items. He has a chance to pick out the good stuff that's worth something. The rest of it just goes to Goodwill. We sort of teamed up because I have an eye for antiques. I can resell those items for a hefty price. He's given me lots of stuff that I have already sold. We're pricing a painting right now that might be worth a lot, that if it's an original."

With that certain twinkle in her eyes and almost a purr.

"I think he likes me."

Then she changed her expression. "I don't want to take advantage of him. I feel a little guilty. He wants to keep giving me things."

He knew her well enough. He was reading between the lines, and he knew that she was already committed to using this man. It was so much of her pattern. He had prepared his answer.

"Well, he is a grown man. Besides you are doing him a favor being nice to him. Obviously, he is lonely and wants some company. If he's willing to do these things for you. He's a big boy!"

"That's what I thought, but he's really vulnerable because he misses his wife. You know I think he wants to marry me, and you know where I am on that one. Besides, he's a little too old for me."

With half of a smile. "In fact, we went to the shelter to get him a dog. I thought it would be a good idea if he had companionship."

Michael guessed that this Widower felt he was getting the dog for her. Except he would be the sucker who ended up taking care of the dog. Of course, he knew where this was going. Someday into the future, the Widower would get tired of the dog.

A short time later, she announced. "He gave me twenty-three thousand dollars, so I could pay off my SUV and he gave it to me in cash with no strings attached."

He knew how she managed to do that. She was always moaning and groaning that she didn't have the money to pay for her SUV and that she was in trouble with her payments.

She gave Michael her look of pleasure, pride, conquest. "He asked me if I was a prostitute."

Michael tried to stay neutral over all of this. He was happy when she was happy.

A short time later. "He brought me this new laptop, the top of the line. The salesman said that this computer is so advanced that will last me for a lifetime. I can do almost anything with it."

WHAT//////???? He was laughing to himself because he knew how computers were changing. No computer could be good for a lifetime. It was her overkill. Look at what I have. At this time laptops were a novelty and still very expensive and he knew that this baby cost at least five thousand dollars.

He was surprised how quickly she found a use for this computer. She really wasn't someone who was into emails and stuff, yet she found a dating site.

"I am really having fun. I have gone online pretending that I am a guy and hitting on some really cute chicks."

Chapter 46

Custer's Last Stand

He was all excited because Poppy wanted to get together with him. The only bad thing was that it meant driving all the way up past North Hollywood to Glendale. At least an hour drive with no traffic and in traffic. Who knew? One could never predict travel time on the freeways in this part of LA.

He had been there before, with her! Poppy loved that area because there were so many stores for her to do her shopping. This time the reason for her to be in Glendale was that she was an honored guest. Poppy chose him to be her escort and that made him feel good. She was the honored guest because she had purchased many paintings from this artist. They were not inexpensive pieces, and the artist was honoring her. This was the artist first exhibition on the West Coast.

When he got there, she was right in the middle of all the attendees. She was dressed so beautifully in a dress with such bright colors. The dress just looked exquisite on her, and the colors were bright orange and yellows. They just made her face and now a non-blemished face standout with radiance. She did look gorgeous, and she was a knockout. She seemed to be very happy.

In the middle of the proceedings, Poppy said to him. "You know, I need to take off. I have an important supper engagement with Ashley. I told her I didn't want to host this supper, but she insisted that I be there. She thinks I am the greatest hostess she has ever met. There are going to be a lot of important people there. She told me I would be just so perfect for this get together."

And she added with resigning jester. "She told me.___ She really needed me to be there."

He was shocked, angry, and disappointed because he assumed that he was going to have the whole evening with her. What hurt the most was that she seemed to be so elated and happy, when she spoke those words (she needs me there). She was somewhere else, and she wasn't there. He felt so lost. He couldn't catch up to her to tell her how he felt about her. Before he could react or say anything, she was gone. He was there alone and embarrassed. He tried to sneak out without attracting anybody's attention. He left and walked for a while. He then noticed there was a nice bar right across the street. He decided to go there and have a bourbon on the rocks. At least till the traffic died down.

He always had to coach the waitress. "I mean ice and bourbon and no water."

If he was at a bar, there wouldn't be a problem, but most often the waitress would get it wrong. Bartenders would always caution him that he wasn't using the correct title for that drink. So, he had learned to be very specific and order ice with Bourbon on top and the emphasis, no water. Even despite his specific instructions, the waitress would bring him, the bourbon mixed with ice and water.

He got his drink, and it had the ice and no water. He only had a couple of sips. It had a bite to it. When there was a bite, he could make the drink last forever. When the bourbon was all gone, he would sip on the ice cubes until he finished every bourbon coated ice cube. He had gotten so accustomed to drinking bourbon that he forgot what Scotch tasted like. The other advantage of a bourbon over a glass of wine, was that he probably could consume three glasses of wine to one bourbon. He was being frugal, as usual, and liked that word better than the other word, cheap. Yes, he got use to be called that, CHEAP! Wine wasn't cheap at nine dollars a glass or up to twenty dollars a glass.

He never liked the taste for bourbon, his preference was scotch. His scotch preference was true only in his younger years. Over the years, he got use to the taste of bourbon. Besides, it was significantly cheaper than most of the other bar drinks. Over the years, mainly because of his cheapness, he would remind people that he wasn't being cheap; he was just being frugal. He resented being referred to as being a cheap Jew. He had 1% Jewishness in him, and he was proud of it. So later in life when they called him a Jew, he felt that this was a big step above being called a Catholic. He started to see it as a great compliment.

He had his drink and he nurtured it ever so slowly. Unfortunately, the alcohol did bring on a pensive mood. One bourbon would wear off very quickly and the depression would fade. He started to realize just how angry he was. He was angry enough to know that this was the last straw, and this was the end. It was the end because he started caring for her. That was what made the difference. Her turning away from him was part of her borderline personality. She was so afraid of abandonment. Borderlines tend to break off relationships before they can get into the feelings of abandonment.

CHAPTER 47

Goodbye Huntington Beach

Hello Tucson

The house was sold, and he had to move out immediately. He moved to Tucson. With the money from the sale, he managed to buy the home that he and Poppy had looked at and almost bought when they were in Tucson, that was the property which was right on the edge of a state preserve.

He wanted to get a Weimaraner to fulfill some unfinished past business. When he was married, he had a Weimaraner that he was attached to. But he was too much of a dog for his family and he had to have them put the dog to sleep. He had gotten this large dog not understanding the impact that he would have on the family. He had been afraid of dogs, and he wanted a large dog thinking that he would help him overcome his fear of dogs.

When he saw this pup, he fell in love with him. He looked so regal with his muscular body, looking hairless and with a short stubby tail. He decided to call him, Jaycoff. Jaycoff sounded Russian to him and reminded him of the aristocrats who were exiled from Russian after the Communist Revolution.

He wasn't prepared to take proper care of a dog that would eventually weigh about eighty pounds. He was temperamental and a high maintenance dog. Michael had assumed that his family would take up the slack, but the dog demanded a lot more attention than what he could give him. He was a hunting dog and needed lots of daily exercise otherwise he became mischievous. He was wonderful on camping trips. And Michael never felt more protected than when he was with Jaycoff.

His wife was a working mother, a nurse, and he was a travelling salesman. The kids didn't want to help in taking care of him. He did feel betrayed by his family and in some ways, he felt they were jealous of the dog. After five years of living with Jaycoff, his wife finally convinced him that he they needed to have someone adopt Jaycoff. Not something he wanted to do, but to keep the peace, it was the only thing he could do to appease her.

The dog was really handful. He bit a couple of people. Even though they had built a run for him, he would whine while he was in it and that annoyed the neighbors. They bought a house with a park that was only a few feet from the house, but Jaycoff wasn't happy unless he could run there for a couple of hours a day. Jaycoff was only happy when the family were with him. They finally found someone willing to take care of him. Unfortunately, he ran away from them and headed back to his home.

He got a call one day and a woman was on the phone. "My brother found this dog on the beach with a name tag and your phone number. My brother wants to keep him, but I felt it was my duty to call you and let you know that we found him."

He was about a mile away from his home. Michael's heart jumped, sick in the heart, remembering the good times the family and the dog had at the beach. He had too many conversations with his wife to know that he couldn't take Jaycoff back.

"I can't take him back. My wife asked me to find a new home for him. Do you think your brother can take care of him?"

"Yes, he loves him, and my brother is very responsible."

Sometime later he received a call from the animal shelter.

"We found your dog and you have 48 hours to claim him otherwise we will have to put him to sleep."

He was in total shock. Everyone had adjusted to not having him there and as far as everyone was concerned, he was living with someone and was happy. Michael knew that it was unfair to his wife to have make the decision. There was only one way. He would have to let them put him to sleep. His wife was now working almost full time. The kids weren't old enough. The dog just couldn't be left alone, and they certainly didn't have to money to place him a kennel while they worked. There just wasn't any other way. He was a lot of dog. He said nothing but his son overheard the conversation and later told his mother.

She went to the shelter. Everyone there tried to convince her that he was a such a beautiful specimen, and it would be ashamed to put him down. She was a nurse, and she knew her duty. She stayed by him as he went to sleep. She later told her son that it was the hardest thing that she ever had to do, and she felt as if she was having a heart attack.

Michael knew that this was the end of their marriage. He felt like he was in a hot air balloon and the only thing to keep it afloat was to drop ballast and Jaycoff was the first to go. They had lived with Jaycoff for five years and he felt the dog didn't deserve that kind of fate. Michael was very upset and felt he should have been stronger and taken the dog back.

So now in this new place and with lots of land around him. He was going to pay his penance. He was going to get another Weimaraner. He was smart enough to know that he didn't want to start all over with a pup. Michael knew he wasn't going to live forever so he wanted to get a dog that would age with him. He started contacting breeders. He thought they might know of someone who passed on or couldn't care for a dog any longer and wanted a good home for their dog.

It didn't take too long. When he saw this dog, they instantly bonded. He believed that animals have a lot of ESP. He had found his five-year-old, healthy male Weimaraner. So, with this new dog which he called Jaycoff. He was going to make it up somehow to the first Jaycoff. This time he would be smart and hire someone to help him with the dog and he would let Jaycoff exercise every day in the adjacent magnificent park. The wilderness, next door, that flat desert, the beautiful saguaro cactus and all that land that surrounded his place. He so enjoyed watching the dog enjoying himself and in so many ways it just made him feel good.

He finally bought a Smith and Weston like the one Poppy showed him. He practiced with it every day and became very proficient with it. He worried that Jaycoff might be attacked by a snake. He trained him to stay away from all the snakes. But just in case, and there were a few. He shot in front of them; they would slither away and Jaycoff learned to let them go.

He had his little farm. With his vegetables and all and of his precious marijuana plants. He sure loved his little garden. Only once did he have to kill an animal. A coyote got to close to his chickens, and he was afraid that Jaycoff would go after the coyote, so he shot the coyote.

He realized now that a dog like Jaycoff, a Weimaraner, was happy with one master and was very obedient. It had all been his fault in having a beautiful animal like that was shared with children.

He understood now that one of the problems was that the original Jaycoff thought he was one of the kids.

He learned that Weimaraner really need one master and all the attention that a dog can get from that one person. He had made a mistake and he felt good that he was able in a way to relive what he should have done in the first place. But he had not been ready for a divorce back then and he did the best he could have done. It was all a very painful experience. Fortunately, he lived long enough to be able to forgive himself. We make many wrong decisions in our earlier life. Sometimes, it is just inexperience.

Chapter 48

A Month's Worth Of Heroine

Poppy called him some months later, after he moved to Tucson. "Guess what? That ring was appraised for over twelve thousand dollars by one of my friends who owns a pawn shop. Well, it gave me a month's worth of heroine."

He didn't know whether to believe her. Did she really sell the ring to pay for heroine? She had told him a similar lie before about the ring being stolen. He knew that she had experimented with heroine before. He remembered her telling him.

"Man, one time I tried to shoot it through a blood vessel under my tongue. I was trying to avoid tracks. I 'll never do that again. It really hurt."

Another time she told him. "I can't get addicted to that stuff. I know how to kick it."

He knew nothing about heroine. As an ex-pharmaceutical salesman, he had a great deal of respect for drugs and their side effects. Used at the proper dosage they could perform miracles.

Addiction was something else. He had learned a long time ago that an experiment was done on dogs using addictive drugs. The dogs never got addicted because they were never given increased amounts of the drugs. The human body adapts to drugs and require ever increasing amount to get to the   desired effect. He also learned when he did his residency, that addict's body have their own preferences. Some patients preferred alcohol, marijuana, sedatives, or stimulants. He had one patient, young sixteen-year-old who loved angel dust. He knew in Poppy's case; she loved opioids and probably needed them.

Whether she was lying or not, it didn't make any difference to him. He wasn't sure why she was telling him this story. Maybe she was pleased because Michael was able to cough up the six thousand for something that had a real value of twelve thousand. Maybe she was patting herself on her back that she was such a sharp buyer, that she was the one who picked out the ring. I guess, in a way, she was bragging that she found another good deal. The engagement ring was nothing more than a commodity to her and could be converted easily into cash.

But by now, he was numb to her tricks. She proved that she was survivor. She was a businessperson; something every American should be. Something that every American should be proud of. She was a true capitalist and money ruled. In her way, she was telling him that the slate was now wiped clean. The balance was now, zero. He was happy with that thought. He liked balance, YIN AND YANG, the algebraic equal sign, and the entropy of the universe.

THE END

Michael Goes Back To Huntington Beach

Michael passed on his 85th year from pneumonia in Tucson, Arizona. Poppy was his last affaire. Joe took an early retirement from the Los Angeles Police Department but a year later, he had a severe stroke. Poppy became his caregiver, but he never completely recovered and was very dependent on Poppy. Even while with Joe, Poppy carried on her discrete affaires with men as well as women. Her poems finally were published, and they were popular with a strong following from the LGBT Community. Poppy passed on at a ripe old age of ninety-three from natural causes, in spite of so many of her imagined diseases.

The surf was up. Walter was only fifteen minutes from Beachwalk where he and his dad both enjoyed all those years together when Huntington Beach was still a small sleepy beach town. It wasn't that way anymore and now their little townhouse was worth over a million dollars. Edward took the Urn, with the waves pounding him; he went as far as he could. With the surf breaking just right, he spread the ashes out on the next wave.

"Go ahead Dad. Ride it all the way in. In the same way you lived your life."